MULE
Maze Shoot

Copyright © Maze Shoot 2021

All rights reserved.
No part of this publication may be reproduced, stored electronically, or transmitted in any form or by any means without the prior permission, in writing, of the author.

The following story, and the events and characters contained within it, are fictitious and not based on any actual events or individuals. Locations may have been altered to suit the story.

First published in 2018

Thank you

Thank you, to the colleagues who stopped me on my way out of the door, on my last day at work, to wish me good luck.

You saved my life.

Thank you, to the guy in the car in front of me who struggled with his ticket at the car park barrier for five minutes.

You saved my life.

Thank you, to the learner driver who stalled trying to pull away on the Rodbourne Bridges roundabout.

You saved my life.

You'll probably never know it, but if you hadn't all delayed me on my way home from work on the last day of November, I would have been at home when it happened. I would have been parking my car on my drive, walking to my front door, entering my hallway, putting my rucksack and keys down in the kitchen.

I would have been dead!

Instead you conspired to ensure that I was behind the petrol tanker, not in front of it.

The leaving presentation had been the usual embarrassing ordeal. This was only my second one on the receiving end but I'd had to present a fair amount of leaving gifts over the past few months so I knew the drill.

With so many staff leaving recently, we'd dispensed with the usual routine of cards and collections. After all, it would have become expensive for the last ones remaining if they'd contributed to every single leaving gift. Instead, we did it secret-Santa style. Those of us who were going put our names into a hat and we each pulled out the person for whom we were to spend a whole ten pounds on a leaving gift. Harry from IT seemed to be exceptionally pleased with the Bluetooth shower speaker and disco lights that had been my present to him.

I, too, was very pleased with my gardening set, even if it was bright pink. They were good quality tools. A trowel, hand fork and garden claw, all made from robust steel with rubberised handles, according to the box. Lizzie from reception raised her eyebrows at the garden claw. Turning it over in her hands and using it to scratch first her head and then her backside, she had to ask what it was for. I explained that it was a bit like a small rake. The sharp prongs, angled at 90 degrees, allowed you to pull it through the soil removing weeds and large stones so it would be particularly handy for the vegetable garden. Gemma from Human Resources pointed out that the colour would, at least, mean that the tools wouldn't get lost in the garden.

I'd shaken hands with all of the remaining team as I left the office. It was touching that they all seemed genuinely sad that I was going.

I vaguely recognised the guy from the office downstairs at the car park barrier. He was in his Fiat Barchetta, so it was little wonder he struggled to put his card in the slot. The Barchetta is a left hand drive. He'd tried at first to reach across the passenger seat but, realising his arms weren't long enough, he'd ended up getting out and walking round. Then had to dash back to the driver's side before the barrier closed. The idiot behind me hooted so I gave him my best Paddington Bear stare in my driver's mirror. Couldn't he wait just a couple of minutes? Why did he have to be so rude? I wasn't in any hurry. I had plenty of time now.

But it was you, dear learner driver, who introduced me to Markus Stalbrigg and his Eco-fuelle tanker. That was surely a contradiction in terms, a petrol company calling themselves Eco-fuelle? OK, so I should have felt ashamed, I had driven the two miles to the office, that morning, instead of walking. But it had been raining and it was my last day at work so I had my personal effects to bring home. At least that was my excuse; besides, if I had walked, I wouldn't even have my car now. It would have been parked on my drive when…

Not that I knew who Markus Stalbrigg was then, of course. I wouldn't find out who he was until after he was dead.

I'd grinned to myself as the learner stalled attempting to pull onto the roundabout. I'd done it so many times when I'd been learning to drive. I could wait, there was no point making him panic even more by hassling him from behind. I don't understand people who do that. It only slows them down in the long run.

The traffic lights changed on the approach from the east and cars and lorries swarmed around from our right. We waited for the deluge to abate. The last vehicle round was Markus in his toothpaste tube on wheels. He was driving oddly, even then but, at the time, I'd put it down to a stranger not knowing the area with an out-of-date sat nav. Had it been updated with the new roundabout layout? We both pulled onto the roundabout behind him. You, dear learner-driver-saviour, went left, towards the motorway, I was heading straight on and Markus appeared to be going back the way he had come so I tried to sneak past him on his inside. It was a mistake. The lorry veered off suddenly, in my direction, so I had to break sharply to let him past. He was going rather fast for someone who didn't appear to know where he was going.

My concerns mounted all the way along Chene Street. One minute he was dawdling, no more than 10 miles an hour, the next he was accelerating madly. I let him go on ahead when his speed climbed over the limit. It's a built up area, my built up area. These are my neighbours. I'm not prepared to be the one responsible for running over their kids, or squashing their grannies, so I stuck, boringly, to the speed limit. Deal with it; it's the way I am, a boring, middle-aged Chartered Accountant, who sticks to the speed limit.

He must have slowed down at some point because I caught up with him near the roundabout with Home Street, but he was travelling way too fast, again, by the time he reached the junction with Gloucester Road. It's a tight turn, a crossroads where two busy streets meet, built in a time when cars were a novelty and goods were delivered on slow, lumbering, horse-drawn carts, not in

50ft long metal tubes. Houses and shops line a narrow pavement allowing no space to widen the road.

He thundered up to the junction then braked at the last minute. The trailer slewed across the road. What was he doing? Where was he going? He didn't make the right turn cleanly, mounting the kerb and hitting the rubbish bin outside Farmer's Fayre. The tanker wobbled but stayed upright.

I followed him at a distance. I wasn't going to end up wrapped around his exhaust pipe. Then, at the crossing outside the post office he leant his head out of the window and threw up. He threw up but he continued driving. It was too much; how could I consider myself a responsible citizen if I didn't do something? I grabbed my phone from the centre console and started to dial 999 as I pulled on to the drive of Gordon and Bev's house. I wanted to get the police to pull him over. Stop him before he did any real damage. Before he hurt anyone…

It's true what they say about time slowing down. I watched in horror, fascinated as the trailer fishtailed, first left, then right, then left again. On the last swing, it caused the cab to slew across to the right spinning the entire lorry so that it was pointing directly at the house. Even though I was sitting in my car, three doors down on the opposite side of the road, the dispatcher heard the crash as she answered the phone.

"Emergency, which servi….. Wow – what was that bang? Are you OK? … What just happened? ……… Are you there? … Hello! Are you OK?   Hello!   Hello!"

"I'm here" I replied, eventually, quietly. "I'm..., I'm..., I'm fine... " I could barely get the words out.

"You just heard a lorry crashing into a house. Erm..., we need police, ambulance and er... and fire please." No reason not to be polite. "The address is 140 Gloucester Road, Swindon. About a hundred yards east of the junction with Chene Street."

There was a moment's pause and then the dispatcher said: "OK, you're doing really well. I've requested the police, fire brigade and ambulance. Now I need a few more details. Can I take your name please?"

"It's Sam Wilston."
"Sam Wilson." She repeated.
"Wilston – with a 'T'."

Get used to it, I've had to. I've had a lifetime of my name being mispronounced and misspelled.

"OK, Sam, we may need to contact you for a witness statement, can I take your address, please?"
"It's a petrol tanker, you'd better warn the fire service that they'll need specialist equipment."
"Good, thanks for that, I've made a note. Is this your mobile number? We may need to contact you again."
"Yes, this is the best number for me." No point giving them my home phone number, not now.
"OK, now I need your address as well." I just knew I had to tell her something first.
"Oh, and tell them that there isn't anybody in the house. No need for them to risk hurting themselves searching."

"OK, are you sure about that? I still need your address."

"My address? My address is 140 Gloucester Road, Swindon. That's why I'm sure there's no one in the house. It's my house." At that point I broke down.

A lifetime passed and then I became dimly aware of a small voice coming from my lap "Sam, Sam, are you there? Are you OK? Sam?" Then a tapping somewhere near my right ear. Tap, tap, tap…

Suddenly the driver door opened and a hand landed on my shoulder.

"Are you Sam Wilson?" I looked up into the eyes of a toddler in police uniform. It was true; they really are getting younger every day. There are times when, I just don't bother correcting the mispronunciation of my surname. This was one of them.

"Sam? I'm PC William Barrett." Why are all babies named after my grandparents these days? Grandpa had been a William.

I blinked, suddenly embarrassed that my eyes were streaming and my face was wet. The voice in my lap was still trying to get my attention: "Sam, is someone there with you?"

PC William Barrett picked up the phone and spoke into it for a minute or two. Then he handed the phone back to me. The voice had stopped. The despatcher, satisfied that I was now in safe hands, had hung up.

I looked straight past him at the petrol tanker parked in my living room. It was as if the house had just opened its mouth and tried to swallow the lorry whole but it had become stuck in its throat. That must be what I look like, when I'm really hungry and I try to bite off too much hot dog in one go.

"Are you ok, Sam?" PC William Barrett repeated. I nodded. I was physically fine but my hands were shaking. I looked down and noticed that he had his hand around my right wrist; he was checking my pulse. On the other side of the road, his partner was trying to move on the people who were stopping to look and sort out the traffic trying to get past. Rush hour was building and there was a petrol tanker parked in my house that could explode any moment. Surely they should be cordoning off the area, evacuating the neighbours, moving everyone to a safe distance. But, of course, instead of doing that, here was the first officer on the scene, babysitting a weeping homeowner. Shouldn't he be checking on the lorry driver?

I lifted my shoulders and took a deep breath. "Actually, I'm OK. You have things you need to be doing."

"We are going to have to clear the area, are you ok to drive?"

"Yes, yes, I'm OK."

"Do you have somewhere you can go? You should stay with someone, it's best if you're not on your own for a while."

"Yes and yes." I'd already lied to police once in the last five minutes; I really shouldn't lie to them again.

No, I wasn't all right.
No, I didn't have anywhere to go.
No, I didn't have anybody to stay with.

My stomach answered the somewhere to go question. I was hungry, normality was returning fast, so the first place was Pizza Hut then Asda. This was going to be a big shop.

Two hours later and the traffic was the worst I'd seen in Swindon. Gloucester Road was shut along its entire length, as they weren't taking any chances with that lorry. The normality of a pizza and shopping had done what it needed to do. Life carried on and so did I. I'd been surprised that nobody in Asda had mentioned the terrible accident. No whispered conversations around the bottled water. No checkout operators gathering around the supervisor's desk pointing at me and nudging each other. Part of me wanted to shout "Don't you know who I am? I'm the one who's just had a lorry parked in my living room! Did you hear me?" But the boring accountant in me just said, "Shut up, keep quiet, get on with your shopping."

School Field

School Field had to be the most optimistic name you could give to the triangular piece of scruffy land, orphaned and lonely at the end of my garden. I'd bought the house on Gloucester Road with E.J. about 10 years earlier. At the time it was a more generous house than we could have afforded anywhere else. The busy main road held back its value making it attainable without a huge mortgage. After liquidating my mother's estate and paying out her charitable bequests, I'd had just enough to put down a sizeable deposit on 140. The noisy road was the compromise that Kirsty and Phil kept telling us was always needed. I'd grown up under the flight path of what had been the Lyneham Air force Base; if I could sleep through the noise of jets taking off, I would soon get used to the noise of the cars.

One of the attractions of the location was the fact that it wasn't overlooked at the back. A dense hedge separated the end of the garden from a primary school and community centre and the only noise from that direction was the happy sound of children playing. field.

Five years ago the primary school and community centre had been knocked down and replaced by the Home Street Academy. Part of the deal on the planning permission was that a new entrance drive be built taking the cars into the school directly off a new roundabout on Home Street. This left a quarter of an acre, adjoining the end of my garden, stranded on the other side of the new access road to the main school.

Swindon Borough Council, which had donated the land on which the Academy was constructed, had planned to build a dozen homes on the site to generate funds that could be used to offset the worst of the austerity cuts. There was one small obstacle that the Council's officials, highly paid solicitors and over qualified surveyors had overlooked. There existed a covenant on the land that prevented it from ever being built on.

I knew about the covenant as it extended to a small corner of my own garden. My solicitor had spent half an hour and a good hundred pounds, explaining what it meant when I'd bought 140.

My house formed part of an estate built in the 1930's in the classic style of the era. Detached three-bedroom houses and semi-detached two-bedroom houses with modest gardens, clustered around a small "village centre" of a pub and shops with the school just around the corner. When the estate was built, all of the services: gas, electricity, water, and sewerage, were carried in conduits through this piece of the school's playing field to the road where they joined the mains. The various service companies, joined in later years by telecoms providers and cable companies, had placed a legal restriction, known as a covenant, on the land stating that not only could nothing be built on it, but also that no trees or plants be allowed to grow roots exceeding six feet long in case they damaged the conduits. The Council had realised that instead of owning a piece of valuable building land, they now owned a liability. They couldn't even leave it to become a wildlife area as they would have to ensure that it was mowed and kept clear of invading trees. It wasn't a cunning plan given the financial cuts they needed to make.

They'd put the plot up for auction. I'd had a dream of growing my own food and keeping a few chickens and pigs. It had seemed like such a good idea after watching the complete re-runs of "The Good Life" on Dave. I put in an offer prior to auction but it was turned down. So I went to the auction and, surprise, surprise, was the only person there who was interested. Any serious property developers had done their homework and realised what a turkey the plot was. That was an idea, how about a couple of turkeys for Christmas? I ended up paying ten grand less than my previous offer and there was nothing the Council could do. The saving wouldn't matter in the long run; I would end up paying it back in council tax over the next ten years.

The construction company that had built the school had left a portakabin on site. Previously used as a site office for the builders, it was a decent 24 feet long by 12 feet wide. Inside, there was a main room, the full 12-foot width by 15 feet long. A door opened from there into a reasonable kitchen area, with sink, fridge and several cupboards, off which was a good-sized cloakroom. I took over the separate electricity and water contracts and it was useful to have a toilet and sink in the area that was now my kitchen garden with vegetable beds, a chicken run and a fruit cage. The pigs and the turkeys hadn't quite yet materialised.

I had planned to turn the cabin into a workshop and garden shed but Alan and Rhona had overtaken my plans. Alan's my cousin, son of my Mother's sister, Alison and her husband, Barry. Six months older than me, Alan was more like a big brother. We were in the same year at school and I'd introduced him to my classmate Rhona. Alan was a petrol head. He loved anything automotive and earned himself an apprenticeship at Honda. He and

Rhona bought a house not far from Barry and Alison's house in Lyneham and Rhona became a teacher. For many years they'd been happy, comfortable, living the dream, but Alan had a problem with alcohol. Shortly after I bought School Field he lost his driving license and subsequently lost his job. He and Rhona responded by renting their house out and heading off around the world for a year so. All of their furniture and possessions ended up being stored in my portakabin. But when the year was up, Rhona was back without Alan. He'd chosen to join a project building a medical facility in a remote area of Borneo but Rhona needed a home, her job, her family. They sold the house, divided the money and she took a flat in Cirencester, picking out the possessions she wanted and the furniture she had space for.

Some things were left behind including a rather nice Victorian mahogany linen press, a microwave, a single futon-style chair bed and a sewing machine. I e-mailed Alan and he said to get rid of them, but asked me first to check the secret drawer at the bottom of the linen press. The main drawer wasn't the full depth and tucked in behind it was a second, secret drawer. They had left some, er, 'intimate' photographs in that drawer and he didn't want them getting into anyone else's hands. He needn't have worried; Rhona had cleared them out.

I dumped my shopping bags on the floor of the portakabin and headed straight back out. There was one thing I needed to do as soon as I got home.

I hadn't been too worried about Philpot; he's an outdoor cat. The tiny ginger pompom, that had made a home with me about six years ago, had grown into a fine large tom. If I were at home, he would be alongside me but when I was out of the house, he spent his time in his favourite tree between the kitchen garden and the house garden.

When School Field was initially divided off from the rest of the Academy land, the Council had surrounded it with an eight-foot high chain link fence with a gated entrance off the school access drive. I had cut a hole in a small section of the fence at one end of the boundary with my garden so that I could move between the two pieces of land but I'd decided to leave the rest of the fence as it made an excellent trellis. Now, five years later, it was supporting blackberries loganberries, roses and two grape vines that, together, made the land private from interested eyes. An old dwarf apple tree with a bent elbow on the field side of the fence, just small enough not to breach the terms of the covenant, provided a perfect place for Philpot to hide and keep watch on both the garden and School Field. As soon as I headed outside, Philpot was there. He was clearly unhappy at the activity around the house. Peering through the fence, I could see that the police had erected a marquee over part of the house and a large portion of the garden to protect the evidence from the weather and prying eyes. Nothing to see here! I headed back into the cabin with Philpot.

Once Rhona had retrieved their possessions, I'd made a start on fulfilling my dream for the cabin. It now housed my large collection of DIY tools, mainly in the kitchen cabinets. The gardening tools were hanging on nails in a space in the corner of the cloakroom and a pillar drill, circular saw and a small lathe occupied the main room, alongside the futon and the linen press, which made a great storage unit for the large selection of odd screws, bolts, door handles, and other, assorted items that might come in useful later. You could say that I'm a bit of a hoarder.

It was all a bit dusty and cobwebby. I won't pretend to be the most house-proud person in the world and the cabin wasn't somewhere I entertained, so it occasionally got swept out but, otherwise, the wildlife that found its way in was allowed to stay. I looked around and decided that there wasn't anything that would eat me tonight. I'd make a start on turning it into a temporary home tomorrow.

I opened the shopping bags and pulled out the new duvet and bed linen set bought during my shopping trip and a packet of food for Philpot. There was a picnic set in one of the cupboards somewhere, that would do the two of us as a dinner service for now.

My jacket pocket vibrated; it was the police; Detective Keith Washington calling my mobile. He wanted to talk to me about the accident. Would I mind giving a statement? It would be really helpful if I could go to Gable Cross police station right now. Could I get myself there or did they need to send a car? The idea of a police car turning up outside the entrance to the Academy and carting me off would have the Parents' Association up in arms. There were still the odd mutterings about the sale of the land; there were certain people who thought that the land should have been available for the kiddies to play on, despite the five and a half acres of playing fields that the school already owned.

I hadn't expected that giving a statement, as a witness, would take so long. We must have gone over the incident four or five times, even though the interview was being filmed so that they could dissect my responses later. Detective Keith was clearly a suspicious character and I began to get the feeling that he thought I'd had something to do with the accident.

Q. Why did I start to dial 999 before I knew that the lorry was going to crash?
A. Because the lorry was being driven dangerously and I was hoping the police could stop it.

Q. Was I driving when I dialled?
A. No. I'd pulled onto my neighbours' drive as I made the call.

Q. Did I know the driver?
A. Er, no, why would you think I did?

Q. Did I think it was a coincidence that I was following the lorry that crashed into my house?
A. I'm lucky I was following it. If I hadn't been late getting home, I would have been in the house when it hit. It would have killed me.

Q. Where did I go after leaving the crash site?
A. Pizza Hut and Asda.

Q. That was an odd choice of destination. Why go there?
A. Because I was hungry and I could see that I wouldn't be able to get to any of my things so I needed to buy essentials.

Q. Why was I so calm about what had happened?
A. Because I'm a boring, middle-aged Chartered Accountant who is used to dealing with stress.

Q. How could I afford a house like that on my own?
A. Because I'm a boring, middle-aged Charted Accountant who is used to dealing with a stressful but well paid job.

Q. Is the house insured? Will I get a big pay out?

A. I hope so, I'll need to rebuild. But I imagine the insurance company will only reimburse me for my losses, I'm not exactly viewing this as a lottery win.

Q. Do I have any money worries?
A. No. If I couldn't manage my own finances, I'd be a rubbish accountant.

Q. Surely I must be a bit worried about money if I've just been made redundant?
A. No, I was given a good redundancy package and I have some private income. I should be able to manage for a few weeks until I can get a new job.

Rinse and repeat, twice.

It was nearly midnight when I got home and I was tired and more than a bit annoyed at the insinuation that I had somehow been involved in the crash in order to claim the insurance.

To take my mind off the events of the evening, I searched for a diversion. I kept an old netbook computer in one of the cupboards, it had a few films downloaded and some music that I played while I was pottering in the workshop. That would do for entertainment. What else did I need? I bet there were over a billion people on this planet that would think that my cabin was a palace. I had plenty of time to make it comfortable and there'd be masses of inspiration online. I pulled out the futon and squeezed it into the space between the workbench and the linen press.

I checked e-mails and Facebook. The crash had made it onto the news. Pictures, probably taken from a drone, showed my house from above. The lorry stuck out of the front and the whole area was covered in white foam to suppress any risk of fire.

Philpot and I settled down with popcorn and James Bond and, before I knew it, I was dreaming of log cabins with luxury wet rooms, hand painted kitchens and bed-sitting room furniture made out of re-used doors and floorboards.

The morning after

Tuesday morning and no alarm clock; just joy, as I awoke, that I didn't have to go to work. The realisation that I was, officially jobless and homeless, came a moment later but it didn't dull the warm, satisfying feeling of being able to stay in bed on a Tuesday morning.

But when I opened my eyes, the disappointment kicked in. As I'd drifted off, my mind had cleaned the entire cabin, fitted a shower in the cloakroom, de-cluttered the cupboards, and decorated the interior to a standard that would have earned Pinterest's highest accolade of "Borderline Genius". When I awoke, I realised that I hadn't achieved any of this in my sleep. The dust and mud was still on the floor, the spiders were still catching flies in the corners and the cupboards were still full of dead moths and random DIY equipment.

Philpot, sensing that I was awake, jumped up alongside me. He, on the other hand, clearly had made a start on the housework judging by the cobwebs on his whiskers and the dust in his tail fur. The spider's leg hanging out of his mouth indicated that he'd also appointed himself chief pest controller during the night. My bladder and my stomach were competing to try to persuade me that it was time to get up but it was Philpot that forced me out of bed. It occurred to me that it was best to let him out. I wasn't sure if cats were supposed to eat spiders and I didn't relish the thought of clearing up arachnid induced feline vomit.

My phone buzzed. It was my insurance company. I'd rung them the previous evening from Pizza Hut just after I'd ordered a meat feast and garlic bread. That had been a slightly surreal conversation:

"I'd like to make a claim on my house insurance please, a lorry has crashed into my house."

"Oh my goodness, are you alright? Where are you?"

"I'm fine, thank you. I'm at Pizza Hut."

"Oh, um, that's OK then. When did this happen?"

"About twenty minutes ago."

"Oh – er – OK. Do you have somewhere to stay? We can organise a hotel, although you'd probably be best off staying with someone if you can? You probably shouldn't be on your own tonight."

I'd confirmed that I didn't need a hotel, I had somewhere to stay and yes, I would be better off staying with someone else. I had a feeling that I'd had this conversation before.

The insurers had informed me that a surveyor would contact me the next day to make an appointment to assess the damage.

The text confirmed that the surveyor, K Longthorn, would meet me at the property at 10:00am. My watch showed that I'd slept far later than I'd realised. I had less than an hour to get ready.

As I clearly hadn't fitted the latest luxury spa shower in my sleep, it would have to be a quick wash. Quick, however, isn't that easy when your only form of water heating is a picnic bowl in an old microwave. Note to self, the shower will have to be the type that heats the water and buy a kettle.

Deciding what to wear, however, didn't take long. My entire wardrobe now consisted of the trousers, shirt, jacket, underwear, and boots that I'd been wearing the previous day along with one pair of jeans, a pack of three t-shirts and a selection of underwear bought during my shopping trip. Jeans and a t-shirt with my jacket, it would have to be. I started a shopping list: shower, kettle, and a jumper – it was the first of December, and I was going to get cold.

The morning news feed had more photos. The fuel had been pumped out of the tanker overnight and there were a lot of images, again probably taken by the drone, of the fire engines as well as the police and the fire officers who were working on the site. It was my house, yet I had to watch events unfolding on the news like everyone else. I was the victim but I'd already been reduced to an outside observer.

I set out across the garden towards the house. Philpot was sitting in his tree. He was normally such a laid-back cat, rarely ruffled, not often given to displays of emotion. Even when Felix, the black and white tom from next door, strayed into the garden, Philpot would just give a little growl and let him get on with it. To see Philpot angry and hissing was such a shock that I stopped immediately and peered through the hedge to see what had upset him.

I'd met a good number of surveyors in my time as an amateur property developer so I knew the character climbing over the wreckage of my house wasn't K Longthorn. Becoming a surveyor takes hard work, study, and qualifications. To work on behalf of an insurance company means that you must be presentable and have a certain amount of people skills but this person looked more like someone who had slept outside, rough and ragged, thin and dirty. Probably someone down on their luck searching for loot they could sell. Was he dangerous? Should I stay back and wait for reinforcements or front it out?

I decided to shout from the end of the garden. The intruder would either run away or head towards me. If it were the latter, I'd have time to get to safety. I stepped forward and shouted: "Oi, what are you doing?" He bolted around the side of the house, straight into the chest of PC William. Much to my surprise, the policeman just stood back and let him pass. I was about to complain when PC William put his finger to his lips and waved me forward. We peered around the side of the house together just in time to see the stranger climb on the back of a red motorbike that took off at speed.

"Tom Harris," said PC William. "Known low-life, part-time drug dealer, pretends to be homeless and begs in the underpasses around the town centre. I'm not at all surprised to see him scavenging for loot. What is interesting is what he is doing on the back of a Ducati Diavel."

I have to confess that I'm not an expert on motorbikes. In fact, I can honestly say that I know more about patchwork quilts than I do about motorbikes. I'd prepared an assignment based on Kaffe Fassett for my design degree. But I did know that Ducatis didn't come cheap. Why did I have the distinct impression that the rider, in expensive black leathers, was female?

"Don't worry, my partner has it covered. He's chasing down the registration and has issued a description. We'll find out where they get to." I nodded as if being interested in the bike-riding acquaintances of local drug-dealing, low-life was something I did every day.

The cab of the lorry had knocked out the side wall of the living room and a pile of brick rubble and possessions littered the path between the house and the garage. The corner of the cab poked through the hole and the driver's window was still open. The driver's body, thankfully, had been removed. Fortunately, it looked as if the garage, which was separate to the house, was ok.

As I stepped amongst the rubble, I noticed an SD card, the type you get in digital cameras, tucked under a now-headless blue china cat. Odd, how did that get there? Without thinking I picked it up and popped it in my jeans pocket without PC William noticing. I wasn't trying to tamper with evidence or impede the investigation; I'd pocketed the card for the same reason that Alan didn't want anyone seeing the pictures in the secret drawer in the linen press. I turned and noticed someone talking to Detective Keith and promptly forgot all about the SD card.

The K in K Longthorn stood for Katherine. She was exactly what I expected a surveyor to be. Dressed in spotless black trousers, a waxed jacket and the sort of boots that were just about smart but appeared slightly too heavy, hinting at the steel inserts in the soles, ideal for clambering around building sites. Over her jacket she wore a yellow fluorescent vest with the insurance company's logo on the back. She was almost as tall as me and, under her hard hat, her bob hair cut didn't have a single strand out of place despite the breeze. How do women like Katherine Longthorn keep their hair so perfect?

"Sam Wilston? I'm Katherine Longthorn, independent surveyor acting on behalf of your insurance company." I liked her immediately. Anyone who gets my name right first time gets a gold star in my book. She held her hand out and gave mine a nice hard shake. She was the sort to take charge and, taking my elbow, she ushered me beyond the police crime scene tape before I could say "Hello."

"The police have made it clear that we shouldn't be here. It's still a crime scene. The Scene of Crime Officers" (so that's what SOCO stood for in the TV shows) "are just getting their briefing. They'll be along soon and we mustn't get in their way."

We walked up the road a little way. Looking back, most of my immediate neighbours' houses looked empty. They'd been evacuated for fear of explosion. I'd exchanged texts with most of them over the course of the previous evening and they'd all wanted to know if I was OK? Where was I staying? Did I need anything? I really shouldn't be on my own. This was getting repetitive. I was lucky to have such caring neighbours and I appreciated it. I knew I would need their help in the near future.

Katherine Longthorn and I chatted for a while and then she said she'd need to make a phone call to my insurance company to speak to the underwriters. Where was I staying? She'd meet me there in an hour.

Katherine the Surveyor

With a memory as poor as mine, I struggle to remember faces and names. To help, I mentally classified people according to their relationship to me. In the last 24 hours I'd gained three new acquaintances: PC William, Detective Keith and, for some reason, Katherine Longthorn had become "Katherine the Surveyor".

Katherine the Surveyor's speciality seemed to be non-verbal communication. As she stepped out of the obligatory four-wheel drive at the gate of School Field, a raise of an eyebrow and a tilt of the head was all it took to have me narrating the full story behind my ownership of it. She just nodded at my explanation as if it was the most natural thing in the world.

"Makes sense. The land would only be of value to you or one of the houses down that side." She waved towards the houses along Chene Street that backed onto School Field.

"Your garden isn't huge but this addition makes it a good plot, especially so close to town. You could easily extend your house and still have a garden in proportion."

"I'd need a house to extend." I reminded her as we entered the door of the cabin.

She smiled. "About that. Forensics will be here probably for today and tomorrow so they won't be able to remove the lorry until Thursday at the earliest."

"They're being very thorough for an accident."

"The police believe there's more to it. It looks like there might be a drugs connection. Seems the driver might have been high and they've found some substances hidden inside the vehicle."

Wow, she was good. She'd managed to get all of that out of Detective Keith in a ten-minute meeting. He hadn't said a thing to me about drugs in the three hours we'd spent together the previous evening.

"Once they remove the vehicle, I expect the rest of the house will collapse." She made it sound so straightforward, my house would simply collapse, that's all, nothing serious.

I practised the raised eyebrow in response. It seemed to work.

"At the moment the lorry is propping up the supporting wall in the middle of the house, between the front and back rooms." She explained. "There's no way to safely get inside to prop up the weight above it, so dragging out the lorry will leave the upstairs unsupported." OK, I really didn't need her to draw me a picture, I knew the importance of a supporting wall.

"Your insurance company has asked me to return, once the lorry is out of the way, to re-assess the damage. I can't come back before Monday. What we ought to do is to get some hoarding up as soon as possible to keep people out for their safety and to try to stop a repeat of this morning's activities. Sadly, looting is very common after this sort of event."

It suddenly made sense why PC William had been so interested in the owner of the Ducati. Did the police believe he or she was associated with the drug dealers?

"I'm afraid that you'll get very little back from the contents of the house. Anything that wasn't crushed or damaged by the collision will be destroyed when the rest of the house collapses, or by the foam."

I shot another raised eyebrow – I was getting quite good at this.

"Fire-retardant foam contains solvents to allow it to spread rapidly and prevent fire taking hold. The solvents are quite corrosive, especially to soft furnishings and anything with a painted or varnished surface. Ceramics and metals might be ok, so crockery, cutlery that sort of thing may survive. Silver and gold, however, are soft so will be eaten away if the foam, or a significant amount of the fumes, reach any jewellery. I've seen the entire contents of a jewellery box be reduced to nothing more than dust.

"I'm fairly confident that your insurance company will approve a full pay-out. They'll be looking to recover from the lorry company's insurers so there shouldn't be any problems with your claim. In which case, they'll give you three options. The first, and easiest option is that you authorise your insurance company to rebuild a house as similar as possible to your old one. It will be identical in size and layout and similar in design but be built to modern building standards. You just move back in once the build is complete. The second option is that you work with an architect nominated by your insurance company to build a similar house at the same cost. You can change the layout, size or look of the house but you may have to contribute if it costs more than the rebuild insured value. The last option..."

For some reason, Katherine the Surveyor paused here. She looked around her and nodded as if she knew what the answer was going to be.

"The last option is that you simply get a bank transfer for the full rebuild insured value and you choose what you do. The insurers walk away at that point. You can rebuild yourself or you can move on and sell the plot. Quite a few people do that if they feel their lives have been at risk. They can't bear to live in the same place again. Others choose this option if they have a dream of building their own home." It was her turn to raise her eyebrows. Did she know that I had been dreaming for years of doing just that?

"I also expect you to receive the full insured value for your contents. It'll be up to you to replace them as and when you need to. There is also a sum available to you for costs such as renting somewhere else to live. If you don't spend it, you can choose to use it for the rebuild if you wish. Were you thinking of living here while you rebuild? It may take a year or more so you'd be here over winter."

Although I'd been thinking of doing just that, I guess I'd really assumed that I would move into something more conventional. A few years back I'd bought a large house and converted it into three flats, all of which were currently let. But tenants move on and it was likely that one of the flats would become free at some point in the not too distant future. I'd planned to move in there when the time came. Hearing Katherine ask if I was going to live in the cabin, as if it was the most normal thing to do, made it seem like a real option somehow.

"Well, I'm not sure." I ventured. "There's no bathroom, but I did wonder if I could put a shower in..." I waved my hand vaguely towards the cloakroom.

Katherine got up and walked through to the kitchen. She peered into the cloakroom.

"I can't see why not; plenty of space in there. We often use these cabins as site offices. I'm guessing that was how this came to be here? They can be a bit chilly in the winter." She nodded towards the little electric fire tucked under the workbench.

"A nice wood fired stove would make this very cosy. It wouldn't need to be anything big or expensive. Have it in the middle here, against the kitchen wall so that it heats up the whole cabin. You'd probably get away with one length of twin-wall flue pipe and a roof plate to vent the smoke. You could do the whole thing for less than five hundred pounds and you'll have plenty of wood to keep it going. You can try rescuing the floorboards and the doorframes from the house but they won't be up to much else. That saw of yours...," she nodded towards the circular saw sitting on the bench, "will make short work of chopping it for firewood. Get a flat-top stove and you can cook on it. Save buying a hob."

As she came back into the main room she commented "I volunteered for a year in Borneo building a school." Was there anybody on the planet who hadn't volunteered to build some form of worthy building in Borneo apart from me?

"Lived in a log cabin smaller than this with three other volunteers. We'd have loved a set up like this each."

So that was it then. She'd decided for me that I was going to take the money to build my new house myself and live in the cabin while I was doing it. Didn't really look as if I was going to get a say in the matter.

"Now, you have a mortgage company noted on the insurance?" It seemed to be a question so I confirmed that I did have a mortgage on the house.

"Unfortunately, they usually want their loan repaid when something like this happens." What! I hadn't expected that one. She could clearly tell that I was surprised.

"Yes, they seem to think that knocking down the house on which their loan is secured somehow devalues their security. How much do you owe?"

I told her roughly how much was left on the mortgage.

"Hmmm. The value of the land as a building plot would easily cover that but I doubt they'll see it that way. If they've lent you money on bricks and mortar, that's what they'll want. I'm bound by law to tell them what's happened. I can try to appeal to them but I don't hold out much hope. It shouldn't be a problem, you just re-mortgage when you start your rebuild. You end up in the same position at the end of it all."

"There's only one slight problem – I was made redundant yesterday so I don't have a job. Getting a new mortgage might not be so easy."

"Might not be as hard as you think. Presumably you were going to get another job? Or do you have your own income?" Clearly I wasn't going to get any sympathy from Katherine the Surveyor.

"Remember that your insurance company also does mortgages. Have a word with them when you're ready to start building. They'll have mortgage advisers on hand to help."

"It's alright, thanks, I've already got one of those. He's usually up for a challenge." The reality was that the mortgage on the house had been taken out to buy the flats and my mortgage broker had got a cracking good deal.

"Who's that? I know most of the local mortgage brokers?"

"Toby Statis at LiveHome."

"Knows his stuff for a 14 year old doesn't he?" She laughed. I was taken aback, so far Katherine the Surveyor hadn't shown much sense of humour but I knew exactly what she meant. I'd been somewhat concerned when his predecessor had told me that he was moving on to pastures new and that Toby was taking over. He certainly looked about 14 but every couple of years we met up to look at options for re-mortgaging and each time he seemed to manage to save me a pocketful of cash off my monthly repayments.

"Well, you probably ought to just check with the Council about temporary planning permission to live in this cabin while you rebuild. I can't see them being difficult about it. They know that you can't make this a permanent residence so it should be a formality. They'll probably put a time limit on it but you can realistically argue for five years if you needed it. Have the press been in touch yet?"

I shook my head. This non-verbal communication lark was working well.

"They will. They love it when a house gets demolished. Milk it! You might get some freebies out of it; local businesses offering you new furniture, clothes, that sort of thing. Oh, and don't even think of trying to rescue any food from your old kitchen. The foam is highly toxic. Make sure you mention that when you're interviewed by the news channels and you'll get free fish and chips for life."

Press release

The press certainly did catch up with me. They'd tracked me down via Facebook and, after Katherine the Surveyor had left, I found I had several messages waiting for me. Detective Keith had warned me not to speak to them. I thought it best to ring him for advice on the matter.

"Ah, Sam, glad you called. I wanted to update you on what's happening. There's been a significant development. The preliminary forensics indicates that the driver might have been a drugs mule." I must have expressed surprise as he stopped and then explained: "A drugs mule is someone who carries drugs in their stomachs. They usually swallow them in condoms. The idea is that the drugs pass through the digestive system as the traveller passes through customs and the drugs emerge out of the other end once they've reached their destination. It's generally not a good idea as the condoms can split and the carrier suffers a massive overdose which usually results in death."

"Is that what's happened here?"

"Probably, that's where the evidence is leading us at the moment. The erratic driving, the vomit, it's all pointing that way. We'll know more after the full post-mortem but we need to gather evidence. The Scene of Crime Officers are heading out now to process the forensics. I'm afraid that means we're going to need your house for a while. Where are you staying?"

"I have a cabin I can use," I replied. Katherine the Surveyor's approval of the cabin had given the project legitimacy and I now felt able to admit this was where I was going to stay.

"Did you catch the bike rider?" I asked.

"False plates." Was all he replied. I took that as a no.

"The press have been in touch. They want to interview me."

"OK – well that's not a bad thing. Given the latest development, it'd be good to appeal for anybody who noticed anything out of the ordinary with the driver or the lorry. We might find out where he was coming from. Do you feel comfortable doing an interview?"

I'd done some amateur dramatics at school and college. If I could be in panto (Oh yes I could!), then I could handle a TV interview, although I hadn't expected my 15 minutes of fame to be associated with a petrol tanker that had forced its way into my living room.

He gave me some advice on what I should and shouldn't say and I got in touch with the BBC. A reporter was already in the area. He'd meet me at the police tape and we could go from there.

The reporter, John Miller, was accompanied by a twelve-year old with a camera no bigger than Dad's old video camera. I'd seen Miller doing reports for the local news lots of times. It was true that celebrities, even minor ones, are smaller in the flesh than they appear on screen. Against him, I would appear as a giant. I'm 5'11" without shoes and he couldn't have been more than 5'6".

Twelve-year-old Camera Boy was wandering around looking up at the cloudy sky, peering at the camera screen, pointing the lens towards the police who were beginning to pick around in the debris. The lorry was still poking out like a stick of rock jammed into the newly created mouth where my living room window had once been.

"Sam Wilson?" John made to shake my hand. "It's Wilston with a 'T'," I told you, you'd have to get used to it. I've had nearly 40 years of this. Maybe I'll change my name one day but today isn't that day.

John Miller introduced the camera operator but his name escapes me. After a while, my brain just fills up with too much information and I simply can't take any more in. The last couple of days have exceeded my brain's storage capacity.

We chatted a bit about the interview. He asked if I'd heard any more from the police. I told him that they were going to put out a statement about the driver being a drugs mule. He nodded; he'd already seen the statement. How did he get to see it before I did?

Camera Boy came over. "How about if you both sit on that little wall?" He pointed at the wall between my front drive and Jack and Linda's next door. "I could film from here with the house in the background. The light should be ok for a little while. Could you just take a seat while I check the light and sound settings?"

While we waited, we continued chatting. John Miller said: "I did an in depth piece into drugs mules a few years ago. Spoke to a couple of teenage girls that had been conned into going on the holiday of a lifetime with a couple of guys who they thought of as their boyfriends. When they got there, they found that the only way they'd get back home was if they swallowed all these condoms full of drugs."

I felt sick just thinking about it. I have trouble swallowing an aspirin, the idea of a condom full of drugs made me gag.

"What happened to them?"

"They were extremely lucky. One of the girls got scared, had too much to drink and ended up telling the whole story to a local who worked in the bar of their hotel. The bar hand had a brother in the police and he managed to get the girls out of harm's way while they caught the drug dealers. The girls are in witness protection now but are still terrified that the dealers' gang will catch up with them."

"At least they're alive."

"For sure! A frighteningly high number of these packages leak or burst. It's a terrible way to die. It's not much better if you survive. I interviewed a doctor who'd treated a couple of people that had been overdosed that way and lived. They're both in a serious way now though, brain damage, liver disease, paranoia, delusions, and panic attacks. One's got epilepsy, and the other needs regular dialysis due to kidney damage."

I shivered. It sounded horrendous. I'd heard the term 'drugs mule' on the T.V. but thought it was just something that happened in CSI.

"There was a guy who died recently in Barcelona and another who caused a plane to be diverted to Bermuda – he survived. Apparently the cabin pressure in planes causes the packages to burst. Other times, the stomach acid eats through the outside of the packages, making them leak."

"But they must make lots of money out of it, right? They know the risk."

"Often not. The drugs dealers tend to use poor, gullible, uneducated people who don't know what they're letting themselves in for. As far as the dealers are concerned, the mules are expendable. They lure them in, often with promises of a better life that are never kept. The money is a pittance compared to what the dealers will earn from the drug sales."

Camera Boy wasn't daft; he'd been filming us during our conversation. As I hadn't realised we were being filmed, I hadn't been at all self-conscious. By sitting us on the wall, you couldn't see the height difference and, as I later discovered, he got an excellent view of the SOCO team sifting through the debris of my home over our shoulders while we talked.

John Miller wrapped up with some of the questions that were more along the lines of how I'd anticipated the interview would go. Questions, which bizarrely, ended up at the beginning of the interview in the final cut. I repeated what I'd seen during my journey home, the conversation with the despatcher, the information that the police had given me. I didn't mention Black Leathers and her Ducati, and I certainly didn't mention the SD card, still sitting, forgotten, in the pocket of my jeans.

Then he asked me a question that suddenly made me pause and re-evaluate everything that had happened in the last 24 hours.

"Are you angry at the lorry driver for crashing into your house and destroying your life?"

"Angry at him?" I almost shouted. "Let's get one thing very straight, Markus Stalbrigg was someone's son, quite possibly someone's father, husband, brother, friend. He died trying to earn money to provide a better life for himself and his family than he could do by just being a lorry driver. I still have my life. My possessions are insured and they can be replaced. He can't be replaced. His family and friends have lost him forever. Yes, I'm angry but not at him. I'm angry at the drug dealers who lured him into this, the drug dealers who stood to make lots of money from his ignorance and stupidity."

I looked straight into the camera and for some reason my mouth said out loud what my brain was thinking: "You'd have to be an ass to be a mule!"

The prodigal son

Katherine the Surveyor had been bang on the money when she predicted that I would be inundated with freebies. As soon as my story aired on Points West I started to get messages via Facebook and Twitter offering me furniture, food, clothes, and household items. AnniesPanties offered me a wardrobe full of "specialist" underwear, Tim500 said I could crash at his place as long as I liked, did I mind sharing his waterbed? BlueTooYoo granted me free life membership of their online video library. I decided these offers were best ignored. Normal people offered me normal things: bedding (plain blue, bought for my son but he's a Liverpool fan), a washing machine (it doesn't spin as well as it used to), a dining table (it's a bit scratched but it'd be lovely if it was sanded down and re-varnished), a bookcase (could do with a lick of paint), a cake in the shape of a minion (made for a client's son but the son said it was the wrong minion), an ironing board, an iron, a four foot long chest freezer (but you'd have to collect it). The list seemed endless, but the collecting part was going to be a problem in my boring middle aged accountant's choice of car.

Then Stan and Lydia, two complete strangers from Bristol set up a Just Giving page and money started rolling in. I was flattered but it didn't seem right. I didn't need money or furniture. Everything was insured and I had nowhere to put furniture right now. I carefully worded a polite no thank you for each message: 'I'm so grateful for your offer but, unfortunately, I don't have anywhere to store it right now/can't fit it in the car,' but then AndyTheVanMan made a suggestion that took me in a totally different direction.

"Listen I do house clearances the mrs said I shud offer u whatever u need to get back on u'r feet I said to her that u'd have more stuff offered than u'd space for and she said no problem you could do up and sell anything you didn't want – wat with u not working - maybe go round the car boots or something I said how wud you get it there didnt notice weather you had a car but it'd need to be a big un to take stuff like dining tables to car boots so she said what was I doing with my old van good point Iv just bought myself a new 1 well not new new if you know what I mean but new to me so I thoughts to myself I wonders if you want the old one its MOT runs out in 3 weeks c and it needs more work than I cud do on it but you mite no someone who could fixes it anyways I done want no muny 4 it its yours if you wannit?"

After reading the message three or four times I decided he was offering a me a free van if I knew somebody who could fix it. I was sure I knew just the person.

I suspected that Alan's love of all things automotive had started in the womb. Aunt Alison often said that his first words were "Vroom Vroom". We used to spend our school holidays at our grandparents' farm. Alan's sister, Sarah would be in the house with Gran, helping with the cooking or learning to sew and knit. Alan could always be found in the cab of some tractor or other with Grandpa. I would inevitably be with the cows, feeding the chickens or planting seeds in Gran's vegetable garden. It was an idyllic childhood and I never lost my love of growing food.

Alan fancied the idea of revamping old furniture. He looked over the van and pronounced it repairable, so I accepted it, along with the washing machine that didn't spin as well as it used to, and the wrong minion cake (it seemed a shame for it to go to waste).

It had been a shock to see Alan back home about two weeks before the crash. One minute he was installing plumbing in the back of Borneo and the next minute he was standing on my doorstep. I'd had a short text from Alison, earlier in the day, asking me if I was going to be in that evening as she had some gardening magazines for me. She got them from her neighbour who was given them by her daughter who picked them up from her sister-in-law, who would collect them from her grandmother who was the one person who actually bought them. By the time the magazines got to me they were almost a year out of date so I just kept them until the season returned. Once I'd read them, I passed them on to Gordon, across the road, who, in turn, passed them on to the allotment holders. Nothing gets wasted here.

I opened the door to find Alan standing there with a bag of magazines. After I'd recovered from the shock, I gave him a huge bear hug and dragged him inside.

"What are you doing here? I didn't know you were coming home."

"It was all a bit sudden. It's Mum." Alan looked at me as if deciding how to tell me bad news. I knew immediately what he was going to say.

"Not breast cancer? Oh no? How advanced?"

"Early stages."

My mum had been diagnosed with breast cancer when I was 17. I'd been just about to take my 'A' levels when she had her first operation. It was the reason I'd decided to go to Swindon College, rather than a university further afield, so that I could stay at home and look after her. Swindon College offered design degrees, which suited me. It meant I could travel from Lyneham to Swindon every day with Alan, who'd accepted an apprenticeship at Honda, and Rhona who was studying English and History, also at Swindon College.

After her operation and several chemotherapy sessions, Mum seemed to be doing well but about ten years later, the cancer returned in her lymph nodes. Alison took on the role of primary carer as I was working away.

During the summer holidays at college I'd been offered a work experience place with a firm of accountants in their Swindon office. My work experience had consisted mainly of putting marketing literature together and doing the artwork for client proposals or presentations. I'd loved it. The office was small and there was a real team spirit. I was thrilled when they offered me the chance to train with them after I'd graduated. It didn't occur to me that being an accountant would be very different from the work I'd done during the holidays.

But the Swindon office closed about a year before I qualified and I was transferred to Bristol. I spent about eight years commuting from Lyneham to clients all around the West Country. The money was good but I ended up hating the long hours and the travelling. My boss tried to persuade me to move to Bristol but I needed to stay at home with Mum. Besides, I'd been dating E.J. for a couple of years and we'd talked about moving in together. There was no way that E.J., a country lover, would move to the big city.

Mum's death forced me to re-focus. I handed in my notice, sold her house and found myself a role as Group Financial Controller for the European head office of an American electronics group. The office was close to Central Swindon and designing new business systems, financial controls, and spreadsheets just about satisfied my need to be creative. It wasn't my ideal job but at least it paid well and would be only ten minutes' drive from my new home.

E.J. and I chose 140 Gloucester Road together. It was a compromise. I would have been happier with something smaller and cheaper and closer to the town centre. E.J. wanted larger and grander out in the country. We looked at two-bedroom terraces in town and big four-bedroom detached houses in the surrounding villages. 140 fell slap bang in the middle, three bedrooms but detached. Being 'in need of cosmetic updating', kept the price down but the age of the house meant it came with larger rooms, higher ceilings and more charm than it's modern counterparts. A three-bedroom 1930's house with as much square footage as a four-bedroom house built in the 2000's at the price of a two-bedroom semi in the Cotswolds. We painted together, wall papered together, chose carpets and bathroom tiles together, we extended the kitchen, and added a conservatory together.

Then, just as we were about to start on the garden, E.J. made an announcement. A former lover had been in touch. The marriage that had prevented them from committing to each other had ended. The aristocratically wealthy father who'd insisted on the unsuitable marriage had died. E.J.'s first love was now single, minted, and about to start a £1million restoration of the family castle in Cornwall. Did E.J. want to be a part of the renovation project? Oh yes, E.J. certainly did.

I kept 140 and got Philpot to keep me company. His fur was the same colour as E.J.'s hair but his temperament was completely the opposite. Philpot and I had never rowed. Philpot rarely demanded his own way. Even when his food bowl was empty, he just politely suggested that I refill it by rubbing himself around my legs or gently head butting me.

I'd dated since but nobody had stuck around for long. Rhona had wanted to learn to dance so she dragged Alan and I to a Ceroc lesson. Alan had soon given up but Rhona and I continued to go right up until they left for their round-the-world tour. After a while, I started learning other styles of dance but I carried on going to the monthly Ceroc dances on a Friday night. I took up football again for a while. I'd been in the school team and had done fairly well. But it demanded a level of fitness that I found difficult to maintain, stuck in front of a computer all day at the office, so I dropped it. Besides, I'd found a new love; gardening. I'd enjoyed planting and growing vegetables at the farm but that was always under Gran's strict guidance. Now I could do what I wanted. I could choose what I aspired to grow. I decided where to plant it and how to nurture it. I was in charge and it was my chance to show off. That was why I'd bought School Field.

I offered Alan a drink. "No beer, I'm afraid but some good local cider and there's a bottle of white open in the fridge?"

"Something soft please."

I'd raised one eyebrow, then the other. "Soft?"

"I've been dry for two years now. I've learned my lesson. I can't touch it. I'll stick to soft."

Like all good alcoholics, Alan had kept his drinking problem hidden. He'd always been the first to the bar at college, the one to buy a round or offer a can when you went to his house. He had a way of refilling the glasses so you didn't notice that he'd drunk twice as much as everyone else. He could handle it, so it wasn't as if he was rolling in drunk all the time. We all knew he drank a bit more than average but even Rhona had been honestly surprised when he'd been pulled over and breathalysed.

It had been just before Christmas. The police were doing random breath testing in the mornings. Catching those who'd had too much the night before at the Christmas party and were still suffering the effects. It was bad luck on Alan's part; he'd literally been pulled over at random. Nothing about his driving had given him away. Even the officer who'd pulled him over was surprised at the positive response. So surprised he'd asked Alan to take another test on another machine. Rhona and I were surprised. Barry and Alison had been surprised.

Barry had been home on annual leave, and we'd all been out for a meal to catch up the previous evening. Alan had driven them over to Swindon but Rhona had driven back. Alan was drinking beer with his dad and I had been drinking cider but he'd surely only had as much as Barry and I'd had?

But once caught, Alan admitted what he'd been hiding. He admitted that he needed a whisky in the morning, while Rhona was in the shower, to get him ready for work. He admitted (not to Honda) that he'd been drinking in his car at lunchtime. He admitted that he'd hidden alcohol in the garden shed and he admitted that, when he went jogging, his water bottle contained vodka.

At first, Alan tried hard to cut down on the booze. He avoided it completely during the week, and only drank in moderation at the weekend but the authorities had caught up with him and he lost his driving license. His job at Honda, by that stage, was as a quality control test driver for their new cars, they gave him a choice; change jobs or leave. He joined Alcoholics Anonymous but Rhona refused to accept his illness so it was I who accompanied him to the first few meetings. Then they came up with their plan to travel and he quit Honda.

"I've got some fresh apple juice, would that do?"

"Your own apples?"

I smiled and nodded.

"Let's try it then."

The apples were still a bit young and the juice was sharp. If anything, it made the juice taste a bit more like cider. I quite like it mixed with lemonade, which made it sweeter, or with sparkling water to keep the sharpness.

"That's not half bad. You could almost think it was cider." Pronounced Alan.

"Have you got your license back?"

"No. I managed to get a license in Borneo, and I was hoping that I could use it here until mine came through, but the insurance companies wouldn't touch me."

"Will you get it back?"

"Yes, hopefully, at some stage. I might have to re-sit my test though. Not really sure."

"You mean you haven't looked into it?"

"No."

"Too scared of what the answer might be?"

"Yes."

"Where are you staying?"

"Mum and Dad's for now"

When Barry had been in the RAF, they'd been entitled to staff housing in Lyneham. A spacious, four-bedroom detached house in a gated, tree lined estate opposite the main entrance to the base. When Barry had retired, the RAF had been selling off the houses so Barry and Alison had bought theirs and stayed put. But Barry wasn't used to being home, and certainly wasn't used to being unemployed, so he'd taken a contract training commercial helicopter crews. At first he was based in Yeovil where he'd rented a flat, returning to Lyneham at the weekends. Then he'd taken a contract in Saudi Arabia, followed by Abu Dhabi, and Alison had returned to being a long-distance wife. Only this time she was allowed to visit regularly and travel first class instead of using RAF transporter planes.

Sarah had long since married and moved out so Rhona moved in at first. The arrangement suited them all. Alan and Rhona could save for a deposit on their own place and Alison, when she was at home, wasn't on her own in the big house. Eventually Alan and Rhona bought a two-bedroom terraced, ex-military house around the corner but they'd only managed two years there before they left for good.

"What'll you do?"

"I've spoken to Honda, they want me to go in for an interview. There are some vacancies in the engineering development team. I wouldn't need to drive."

"How will you get there from Lyneham?"

I'd had a horrible feeling that he was going to ask to move in. Gloucester Road is the main route to the Honda factory. It was a bit far to walk but a comfortable cycle ride.

"That's the other thing I need to tell you. Mum and Dad are moving."

"Oh – where to?"

I'd half expected him to say that Alison was moving out to Abu Dhabi or wherever Barry was now working, and that Barry's health insurance would be covering the cost of her treatment in some futuristic top class private hospital. The answer was far more mundane.

"Dad's retiring; properly this time. He'll be home at the end of November. They're putting the house on the market and renting somewhere in East Swindon, close to the hospital and to Honda. If I get the job, I'll be able to cycle to work. Mum won't have far to travel for her chemo."

I'd been relieved. Much as I loved Alan, I'd grown used to my own space. I couldn't imagine sharing a house again but I couldn't imagine saying no to Alan either. After everything that had happened since that conversation, it was a good job. I barely had somewhere for Philpot and myself now, there certainly wouldn't have been space for a house-share.

It was the day before the accident that I had driven Alan to Heathrow to pick up Barry so that their new lives could begin.

Paternal instinct

The police had finished with the lorry and were due to extract it from my living room the following day. The road, which had been partially opened, would be closed again and the neighbours evacuated, again, just in case anything went wrong. Even I'd been told to stay away. I was getting fed up with being a spectator in my own drama but what could I do?

I went back to tidying up the cabin. I pulled tools, decorating equipment and random boxes out of the kitchen cupboards. In one box I found my drone. Dad had bought it for me for Christmas when they first came out. It was a pretty decent one, with a good live-feed camera. I'd used it a couple of times to photograph the garden from above but, like all novelties, it was soon consigned to a cupboard.

I unpacked it and switched it on. The battery was almost flat but it still worked. I had an idea. Perhaps I could watch the drama unfold after all.

I plugged the battery in to charge overnight, ready for the morning while I checked my messages.

Amongst the hundreds of messages was one from Eddie the plumber. Eddie had helped me to convert the flats and was offering to help again when I was ready to rebuild. It reminded me, I needed a shower. I sent a quick message asking what my options were. I knew I'd need an electrician to run a cable direct to from the fuse box. That was all right, I knew just the person. I'd just picked up the phone to make the call when it rang in my hand.

"Hi Dad. I was going to call you later."

"I just wanted to check you were ok? Rosemary said she'd spoken to you yesterday and you were really busy. Is everything alright?"

Alison had been my mother's older sister by a good five years. Both sisters were born in October. Grandpa used to joke that there had only been two snowy winters in the 1950's, one in 1952 and one in 1957. Gran had boxed his ears while Alan had laughed heartily with Grandpa. I'd asked him afterwards why it was funny.

"No idea but Grandpa thought it was funny."

It was Sarah who, being several years older than us, understood about where babies came from and who finally explained the joke. After that, we sniggered embarrassedly every time Grandpa mentioned it.

I'd studied birth order theory briefly at college. My degree included a module on the psychology of design. My tutor also taught other psychology courses and convinced me that I was interested enough to attend. I managed the one on birth order theory and then decided that the time would be better spent at football practice instead.

The theory is that our place in our family governs how we behave. First or only children, like Alison, Sarah and myself, tend to be high-achievers, more academic and choose professional careers, like accountants. Second children tended to be more creative, outgoing and people focussed. Mum and Alison had certainly proved that theory.

Alison had left school at fourteen and, like most young women in Lyneham in the 70's, had taken a job at the base as a typist. She'd studied typing and shorthand at evening class and gained, what Gran had termed 'qualifications'. She'd met the dashing young flight engineer, Barry, and, by the time Mum was 18, Alison had a husband, a daughter, Sarah, and a staff house next to the base.

Mum's response was to head off to London and a degree course in music, which my grandparents dubbed a waste of education, not like Alison's 'qualifications'. But, to make things worse, Mum returned three years later with a baby, me. It wasn't quite the scandal that Gran feared as Mum and Dad had, at least, done the decent thing and married. The fact that they did it in secret in London was bad enough but the worst insult was that Dad's parents, wealthy restaurant owners from Birmingham, had disowned him. They felt that by marrying a farmer's daughter, dad was marrying beneath himself.

Dad was an electrician and a musician. As a drummer that could also rig up the sound system, he was good value and he got a lot of work touring. He and Mum met when she was playing the guitar for a little known punk band that he worked with for a while. They came back to Lyneham to settle down. Dad was touring a lot so it didn't really matter where he was based. Mum wanted to be near home and her parents. Grandpa gave them a small patch of land and an old barn to convert. The conversion was complete by the time I was old enough to remember being there and our life on the farm was fun. But when I was about nine, they sat me down. Dad was going to move away and set up his own electrical firm in Stroud. Why Stroud? Because that was where Sandra lived. Mum and Dad were getting a divorce.

Once again, Dad did the decent thing. Mum kept the barn conversion, even though Dad had done most of the work and paid for the materials, and he also paid a fair maintenance for me. Mum already had a job as a teacher at my school and we did all right until the cancer took hold.

Dad said that he could send one of his guys to look at the cabling for my shower. It shouldn't be a big job. With luck I'd have it fitted and working in a day or so. In the meantime, I would do another shop to get that kettle and the jumper.

I'd forgotten the rush hour traffic so my shopping trip took a lot longer than I'd anticipated. But when I got back, there was something not quite right. Philpot came running straight over when I pulled up at the open gate. He's never normally quite so eager to see me. He likes to play it a bit cool, sauntering over to me, tail in the air but with no great sense of urgency. This time, he walked before me, meowing sharply and criss-crossing in front of my legs, as if he wanted to stop me entering the cabin. Heeding his warning, I looked through the windows before I went in. It seemed ok, but inside, something was off. The cabin smelled vaguely of cigarettes, as if a smoker had been in there. I was sure I'd left the netbook closed, but now it was open. I don't usually leave cupboard doors ajar but there were two like that in the kitchen. I got the feeling that someone had been inside but I couldn't be sure. Nothing appeared to have been taken but in the cloakroom, the tools that were normally on the walls were in an untidy pile on the floor. Had someone been in there or had a large lorry driven past and caused the cabin to shake, knocking the tools off the wall? If someone had got in, how had they done so? The smell of smoke faded but had my nose just got used to it or had I just imagined it in the first place?

The cabin didn't have a lock and key, instead it had one of those old-fashioned number pads fitted to the door where you press the buttons and turn the handle. I hadn't bothered to change the number since I took the cabin over from the builders. It had definitely been locked when I entered the cabin but when I looked at the number pad I realised that the keys that made up the code to unlock it were far dirtier than the others. It wouldn't take a genius to work out what the code was.

I thought about calling the police, but what would they do? Nothing had been stolen, no damage done. I bet they wouldn't even come out. But why break in, if you're not going to steal anything? Perhaps I had nothing of value that they wanted to take. The computer was cheap and old and the tools were bulky. If it was kids looking for quick pickings, they probably decided it wasn't worth bothering. The forensic team were still in the house and garden just the other side of the fence. They may have scared the intruders off. I would leave it. Just change the lock combination and forget about it.

It had been a long day and I was tired and hungry. Dinner and bed beckoned.

Another day

The police had acknowledged that they didn't need to inspect my garage, as it hadn't been touched during the accident. I could use it to store some of my stuff but, if I were going to do up old furniture to sell, I'd need it as a workshop so it couldn't just become a dumping ground.

The hens would have to step up, literally, and make some space. I'd already had a thought about their shed. When I'd been planning to get chickens I'd envisaged a cute little hen house in a patch of green grass but talking to other chicken owners had soon convinced me that wasn't the best idea. They pointed out that when it was wet and cold you wouldn't want to be outside topping up their food and water or collecting their eggs. In the end a friend had offered me a pretty decent second-hand, 10x6 wooden shed. I divided it in half with a piece of old fence panel and a makeshift door. The chickens had the back half, with a pop-hole out into their run, and I used the front half to store their food and other paraphernalia.

But it had occurred to me that the hens didn't need the full height of the back half of the shed. In fact, most of it was wasted, as they couldn't fly. I'd already thought about putting a shelf across, half way up. The chickens could have the top half for nesting in, with a plank outside to help them up from the ground, and I could use the area below for storage. I hadn't needed it before, but now the hen house was going to have to double as a garden shed so time to get on with it.

I had the tools and some leftover timber in the garage so that was my chore for Wednesday. I had already made a start when first Udi, the electrician, turned up, then Eddie the plumber to measure up. By the time they'd both gone it was mid morning and I'd achieved extremely little. I wasn't sorry when Alan rang to ask what I was up to? When I told him he offered to help in exchange for a pie and a pint of that fizzy apple juice followed by a piece of the wrong minion cake.

He, Alison, and Barry had been to view a bungalow in Covingham. It had a loft conversion that Alan could use. They all stopped by the cabin on the way home. Alison took one look at the cabin and pronounced it, "Better than I was expecting. You could make this quite homely with a bit of effort". Hmmm, I'd already put in more than a bit of effort, clearly I needed to try harder.

She did notice the lack of washing machine and immediately scooped up my dirty laundry. "You can have this back when you drop Alan off later." I rather hoped she wasn't holding my clothes to ransom for getting her son back. I didn't have many clothes to spare.

It's funny how some jobs take less than half the time with two people than they would take with one. Putting the shelf in the hen house only took a couple of hours. Alan fiddled about with shelf brackets and batons while I shortened the door that would keep the hens in their area but allow me access to collect the eggs and clean out their bedding. The hens immediately took to the little ladder that I made for them and their new high-rise home. I treated us to a pasty from the bakers on Gloucester Road and, as we walked back, I asked him how it was going at home.

"It's bizarre. At the moment it's still quite new so it feels like a holiday. Dad's only been back a few days so I keep expecting him to disappear again. Mum's still OK, just a bit tired but it'll be very different when she goes into hospital."

"Does she have a date yet?"

"The week after next."

"That's the week before Christmas."

I looked at Alan, he would never admit it but I could see real fear in his eyes. He clearly needed distracting and I had just the thing.

"What needs doing next?" He asked. "Shall we box this stuff up for the shed?" Even better, he'd offered so I didn't need to ask him to help. We spent the rest of the afternoon sorting out and boxing up DIY tools, gardening equipment and general junk. We managed to clear a space in the kitchen for the washing machine and the cloakroom was now devoid of gardening tools, ready for the shower.

As we worked, I mentioned the break-in. Alan asked if it was connected to the crash. It hadn't even occurred to me.

"What makes you say that?"

"Well, you did see that guy looting your house."

"I assumed he was just looking for what he could steal. Why would he come here?"

"If there is a drugs connection, maybe they think you have something of theirs."

" I dunno, what would I have?"

It wasn't until I got home from swapping prodigal son for clean, dry, ironed washing, that I realised what it might be.

As I took off my jeans, the same jeans that I'd been wearing the day before, I put my hand in my pocket and found the SD card. Suddenly I realised it couldn't be mine. Mine was still in the camera that I'd put in a box that very afternoon.

I should have just handed it over to the police. Admitted to the mistake. But, instead, I couldn't resist a peak at what might be so valuable. I dug the camera out of the box but when I went to switch it on the battery was flat. Then I remembered that the old netbook had a card reader. That was flat as well but at least I could plug it in while I used it.

Philpot loved being outside so much that when he was inside, he liked to look out of the window. In the house, his favourite place had been on the arm of the sofa where he could watch all the comings and goings of Gloucester Road out of the living room window. Now he was sitting on a small bookcase underneath the window looking out onto the drive and Home Street.

The netbook took its time to warm up. I decided to use some of my insurance money to buy a new, state of the art, MacBook. I couldn't see how mine would have survived the crash. Even if it had, it was getting old and slow, almost as slow as this netbook.

Eventually the screen lit up and I slotted the card into the reader. There were only 3 images on it: a picture of a piece of paper on which was written a string of letters and numbers; a picture of a sealed box, about the size of a large shoe box of the kind that they use for women's knee-length boots or large sports shoes, and a picture of the same box, open. It contained cash, lots of cash, in a mixture of £5, £10, and £20 notes. I looked back at the written note. At the end was a number 250000. Did that mean £250,000? I really should give that SD card to the police.

I looked back at the picture of the closed box. There was a label on the top, a courier label showing the address. It was addressed to a DirectDeliver locker at the Sainsbury's store on the Oxford Road.

I looked up the DirectDeliver web page. I'd seen the lockers at various locations but didn't know how they worked. Apparently, you could get deliveries sent to one where it could wait for up to a month to be picked up. The label on the box had a collect by date – 30th December. That means that the box had been delivered on the day of the crash. Was that where Markus Stalbrigg was headed? He could get onto the Oxford Road from Gloucester Road but it was a long way around. Should he have picked up the box? Was it his payment for being a mule? But John Miller had said that mules weren't that well paid. Was he picking the money up for his dealer? That would explain why they'd been looking for the card. No, that couldn't be it; he'd been coming from the east, from Oxford direction, when I first met him at Rodbourne Bridges. Why would he head back that way?

Just then, Philpot made a sound, not really a meow. More like a bird chirping. It was the noise he made when he was perched on the arm of the sofa in the house and someone walked up the path to the front door. I wonder what noise he would have made if he'd seen a lorry driving up the front path? The thought stabbed me in the stomach and made me feel sick. What if we'd been in the house when the crash happened? Philpot chirped again and I got up to look out of the window. A red motorbike had parked up on the opposite side of the road. It occurred to me that I'd heard it drive past and stop but hadn't paid any attention. The rider, in black leathers, was walking towards the cabin. Although the rider still had a helmet on, I was convinced she was a woman, the leathers showed off a petite figure.

She saw me looking out of the window and turned around, got back on the bike and rode off. I guessed it was she who'd been in the cabin the previous evening. Somehow it made everything all the more sinister. I would go to the police, but not right now. It was late; I was tired. "Time enough in the morning," I told Philpot and I switched off the netbook hiding it, with the card still in it, in the secret drawer of the linen press under a pile of spare bed linen and towels that Alison had given me.

I was still dithering about going to the police the following morning but other things got in the way. I had to pick up the van and Alan was coming with me to make sure it got home ok. We took it back to Alison's house where she protested about it being dumped on her drive but I think that, secretly, she was pleased that Alan, possibly with Barry's help, would have a project to work on while he was waiting to hear about the job at Honda.

On the way back from collecting the van, we'd picked up the washing machine (it certainly didn't spin as well as it used to) and dropped it off at the cabin so the next job was to plumb it in. I could tell that Alan was torn between helping with the plumbing and starting on the van so I told him that Eddie was coming over to do the shower. If I got stuck plumbing in the washing machine, Eddie could help. I really wanted that van to be in good condition as I'd had a shed load of furniture offered and some of it looked really good.

Detective Keith rang on my way back to say that they would be removing the lorry in the next couple of hours. They were closing Gloucester Road and evacuating the immediate neighbours, just to be on the safe side, but I would be alright if I stayed in the School Field side of the fence. That meant I couldn't watch. I was determined to get a better view of my house as it collapsed and I knew just how to do it.

The drone was completely charged up now and working fine. I was a bit rusty with the controls but I wasn't going to be sending it far. The trouble was that the battery only lasted about half an hour and I didn't know how long the extraction was going to take. As I hovered it over the house, I thought about parking it on the garage roof. The camera didn't use much battery so it could just sit there watching. But the garage roof was too low and I couldn't get a good angle on the front of the house.

I thought about squatting on the roof of the house opposite but, as I didn't really know the new occupants very well, I thought that would be a bit of a cheek. Then, as I hovered around, inspiration struck.

Soon after I moved into the house, the Council had replaced the streetlights along Gloucester Road and for nearly ten years it had shone straight into my bedroom window. I'd had to invest in blackout curtains but, even then, the light still crept in around the top and sides of the curtains. Now it was time for the streetlight to make up for keeping me awake at night. The top was the perfect size for the drone to sit on. It took a few goes but I managed to line up the base of the drone on the top of the light with the camera pointing at my front garden. If I zoomed in, I could see the full detail of the lorry, the hole in the front wall and just about see where the cab had knocked out the side wall. If I zoomed out, I could fit the entire lorry, the police cars and fire engines and part of the road on the screen. I would get a perfect view from here. There was only one slight problem; there was a sunlight sensor on top of the streetlight. The drone sitting on top of it, blocked out the sun and the streetlight had decided it was time to come on. Oh well, it was a dull day; a little extra light to help the workers wouldn't hurt.

Eddie appeared about then so I was distracted for the next three or four hours as we fitted the shower cubicle and the washing machine. I had, honestly, intended to do the washing machine myself but, as Eddie was there, well, these jobs are just so much quicker when a professional does them.

It was getting dark as we finished and Eddie didn't have any other jobs to go on to that day so we stopped for a cider. As well as Philpot's favourite tree, there are three other apple trees in the garden so I always have a glut of apples. A month or so earlier, I had taken a car boot full of them to a small cider company over in West Swindon and received a dozen bottles of their medium sweetness cider as payment. I'd been storing them in the shed as I'd meant to save them for a special occasion. I couldn't think of a more special occasion than watching one's house fall down.

Eddie had done all the plumbing when I converted the flats. We'd met at dancing and Eddie had been free with ideas and suggestions while I was still designing the layouts. The work had been top notch so I'd recommended Eddie a few times to friends. We'd got to know each other reasonably well so it didn't seem at all odd to stop for a drink together. The cider went particularly well with a large slice of the wrong minion.

The drone had been streaming the video footage back to the netbook and I noticed that the screen had gone blank. I checked it back and was relieved to find that it had recorded all of the extraction. We watched it together, laughing as it took five attempts for the tow truck to get the right angle. But we both agreed that we were glad we weren't the ones doing that job. They'd closed the road and evacuated the neighbours just in case there was enough petrol left to cause an explosion. We both hoped the tow truck driver was being paid well for this job.

There were plenty of police and firemen milling around but it was eagle-eyed-Eddie who noticed that, just beyond one of the fire engines, lurked a shadowy figure in black wearing what looked like a motorbike helmet.

Katherine the Surveyor was absolutely correct in her prediction that extracting the lorry would result in the final destruction of the house. It wasn't particularly dramatic. There was no explosion or even a sudden crash. As the lorry started to move, the roof of the house seemed to sag, as if it was sighing, and just slowly crumbled down. The left side of the house, comprising the hallway and kitchen downstairs and the small bedroom and bathroom upstairs, sort of tilted over into the space left by its other half so the house ended up looking lopsided, a bit like a scene from a fairy tale. Made all the more spooky as it was dark by the time this happened and the whole scene was bathed in an eerie orange glow from the streetlights.

The lorry had gone, and the police were starting to clear up their gear, when the drone's battery started to fail. The drone, knowing it only had a few minutes charge left, had tried to return to its control unit, inside the cabin. It was now sitting on the outside step alongside Philpot who was staring at it, as if daring it to move. I swear he had one eyebrow raised when I went to collect it and let him in.

He jumped straight onto Eddie's lap. I was miffed; Philpot rarely sat on my lap, but he took to Eddie for some reason. Lifting Philpot off her lap as she stood up, Eddie just laughed: "Obviously a ladies' cat."

"Cheek!" I retorted, "I think I could make quite a good lady." I spun around and dropped into a mock curtsey, pulling at the seams of my jeans to hold them out as if they were a skirt.

Eddie laughed, "Lady Muck, certainly, dressed like that and have you seen the state of your nails?"

I looked down at my hands. It was true, I'd been so busy gardening, decorating and cleaning, that I had neglected them somewhat. My nails were tattered and torn and had half the garden behind them.

"If you're still thinking of wearing a ball gown to the fancy dress dance on New Year's Eve, you should think about a manicure. Do you have a dress to wear?"

I laughed, "Of course I don't have a dress. What you see is virtually all the clothes I own."

"I could lend you one of mine." She volunteered but the thought made me laugh so hard I cried.

"Thank you for the offer but I'd never get into a dress of yours, you're half my size."

We hugged and I found myself promising to think about getting a manicure as she left. Philpot followed her out and sat on the step watching her leave.

Re-acquaintance

I checked my messages again as I settled into bed. I'd never been so popular. The stream of free items offered by genuine individuals had turned into more of a river of advertisements from local companies offering their services to help me rebuild everything from my house to my love life. I skimmed through but my eye was caught by a message from Isaac Barnes. I'd been at college with Isaac 20 years earlier. He'd been on my design course and we'd been in the same tutorial groups for three or four assignments. I wouldn't say we were particularly friends, but we'd kept in touch through social media and met up at reunions, parties, and a couple of weddings.

Whereas I hadn't really known what I wanted to do when I left college, Isaac was determined to be an art teacher from the start and, after about 15 years working in schools in Southampton, Bournemouth, and Liverpool, he'd returned to Swindon to take up a post at the Home Street Academy. We'd waved at each other a couple of times as he left the car park after work and once he'd stopped for a quick cider in the cabin, while it was still a workshop.

Now he was after a favour. His 16-17 year olds had been tasked with designing a social media campaign about something relevant to their peers. They'd seen my television interview and been inspired by my comment: "You'd have to be an ass to be a mule." They wanted to design a campaign highlighting the dangers and the pitfalls of being a drugs mule. Could I possibly join them for a two-hour lesson on Friday afternoon for a chat about what had happened and help them with their campaign? They would like to interview me for a video clip. There'd be tea and biscuits after the first hour.

Of course I couldn't say no. I didn't have any excuse not to go. It was only next-door, I wasn't working and he offered tea and biscuits. Yet, I had reservations and it wasn't the teenagers that worried me. But, still, I messaged him to say, yes, I could pop in on Friday.

He immediately messaged back to say that he was thinking that I could do a presentation for about an hour (to include a question and answer session) on what had happened and then they would talk about how to plan a campaign for the second hour. I could stay and listen or leave after my presentation. I said that was fine and I'd probably like to stay. I'd done a bit of social media stuff, advertising for the football club so, you never know, I might have something useful to contribute. It did occur to me that my commitment had gone from popping in for a chat and a quick interview to giving a one-hour presentation (to include question and answer session). What was I going to say for an hour, I only had a day and half to prepare.

Overnight, an answer came to me. The real expert on this was the TV reporter, John Miller. The following morning, I messaged him. Could he help? Was there any footage available from the investigation he'd carried out or did he have some facts and figures that I could give them? I hoped he didn't mind me asking but this was for a local school.

He responded later that morning with a link to a download of the video of his investigation. He suggested a twenty-minute section in the middle, which contained the interviews with the teenage girls who'd been lured to the Caribbean and had helped to catch the drug dealers. It wasn't as explicit as some of the other footage and would probably appeal to that age group.

That would take up 20 minutes, I could probably talk about the crash and its aftermath for another 20 minutes and, with a further 20 minutes allowed for the question and answer session, my hour would be complete. I jotted down some bullet point notes and messaged Isaac to let him know my plans. He soon replied to say that he wasn't happy about my contacting the BBC and that I really should have checked with him first. He didn't think the video would be appropriate and it wasn't at all what he'd wanted for the first hour.

I felt as if I'd been kicked in the sternum. Contacting John Miller had been to obtain material for the benefit of the students. He didn't know which school I was going to, so it wasn't as if the BBC would be pushing their cameras through the windows trying to film the students. This was exactly what had caused my reservations about working with Isaac again. At college he'd shown that he considered any idea that wasn't his idea was a bad idea. He obviously hadn't changed.

I, on the other hand, had changed. I was far more mature and wouldn't put up with this sort of behaviour. I messaged back to say that was no problem. If he didn't want my help, I wouldn't be offended. I had plenty I could be doing on Friday afternoon without giving up a couple of hours, for free.

Typically Isaac, there was no apology in his reply, just a comment about my "overreacting". I'd learned long ago that this was in the standard weaponry of a bully. They do something to hurt you and then blame you when you get upset. You're "overreacting" or "too emotional". He went on to say that it would be ok as long as I vetted the video content first as he thought it might be too graphic for the age group. Really, was I that stupid? I felt sorry for his students.

Disaster zone

I headed out towards the house. The police had cleared out and it was all mine now. The insurance company were sending out some contractors to put hoarding around the site to keep looters out and I wanted to check how it was going.

It hadn't occurred to me that the police would have taken down their tents the previous day. They'd been protecting the house and my possessions from the elements but now they were gone and it had rained heavily during the night. With the roof so badly damaged by the crash, everything inside the house and all of the random contents scattered around the garden, were sodden. As I looked around, I realised it was even worse. My possessions, that had been disturbed and scattered as the lorry hit and the house collapsed, had subsequently been trampled under foot and crushed by police boots. Here was some of my design work from my college course, wet and ruined. There were some photographs (old fashioned film variety) of my family when I was a baby. They'd been trampled into the mud. I didn't have the negatives and the photographs of my mum could never be replaced. I was furious. I rang Detective Keith to tell him but just got his voicemail. I was already a victim but the police had made the impact far worse.

Katherine the Surveyor called to check how things were progressing. She got the brunt of my anger but, as soon as I'd finished, I felt guilty about ranting at her. It wasn't her fault, yet she was very sympathetic. She agreed it was unacceptable and offered to check with the insurance company whether this was normal or were the police usually more considerate? She could find out whether I could sue the police for the damage that they'd done but, as we talked, it was clear it would be difficult to prove that they had made the situation worse. I also felt that suing the police would just make me unpopular with my local force and end up costing the taxpayer. What was the point? It didn't stop me feeling less inclined to help the police with their investigation or to tell them about the £250,000 sitting in a cubbyhole over at Sainsbury's.

Katherine the Surveyor said she'd be back out on Monday to assess the final damage but that I could start tidying up if I wanted to. Just be careful around the structure, as it would be unstable. Just as she said that, a large chunk of masonry fell from the living room wall. I decided to fetch my old hard hat from the garage and spent the rest of the day picking up what I could safely reach without getting hit by flying brickwork.

The whole day turned out to be a bit miserable. The spat with Isaac, the damage done by the police, my ranting at Katherine, even the weather joined in by drizzling for most of the day leaving me wet and cold. By then end of the day, I was feeling pretty fed up. Not depressed, or even particularly miserable, but down enough to eat the remaining half of the wrong minion. It was getting a bit stale, to be fair, so needed eating up. I went to bed with yellow fingers and blue lips and far too much sugar in my blood stream.

Friday

If I was cold yesterday, I was colder today. The weather had truly turned wintery and there was a frost when I woke up. It occurred to me that I was still relying on the one, quite old, electric heater to keep the cabin warm and it was probably costing me a fortune in electricity. Katherine the Surveyor had suggested a wood burning stove and it seemed a very sensible solution. I jumped out of bed, had a quick toilet trip, and grabbed some breakfast before getting back into bed with the netbook to research how to fit a stove. I must have drifted off again.

Life on the Gloucester Road had its own rhythm. When I had been working, the first shift at Honda was my alarm clock. The early birds would pass my house at about twenty minutes to six in the morning. That meant that I was properly awake and ready to get up at six o'clock. It also meant that I was awake at that time every weekday, even on my days off. But I'd become very good at turning over and going back to sleep. The traffic along Home Street started much later. The first cars along the entrance road to the school appeared around 7:30 in readiness for breakfast club so I was quickly getting used to waking up much later in the morning.

I didn't have anything planned for the day other than the school visit in the afternoon, so, when I eventually did get up, I occupied myself with general housework. I used my new washing machine and gave the cabin a good clean and tidy. It's amazing how quickly you can do all the housework in such a small space. What would have taken me all morning in a three-bedroom house, now took less than an hour.

I didn't relish any more clearing up on the building site yet so I started to think about the rebuild. I ended up spending the rest of the morning and the early part of the afternoon researching construction methods, eco-homes and local building regulations. I suddenly realised that I only had a few minutes to get ready for school.

I made it to reception just on time. Emily, one of the students, was waiting to sign me in and show me to the classroom. She was surprisingly grown-up for someone so young and, as we walked through the main atrium, she gave me a running commentary about the school. She knew when it had been built, how it had been financed, how it was constructed, how the teaching was organised. I was impressed. I hadn't had the first clue about my school at that age. I could just about find my way from one classroom to another. As we walked through the main hall a sign caught my eye. It simply said 'Examtime' in large letters. I pointed it out to Emily. "Is that to remind you to study?" I asked.

"No." She laughed. "It's the password to the School's Wifi. They change it each term."

School Wifi! We hadn't even had the Internet when I was at school! Boy, did I suddenly feel old.

The session went really well at first. I gave an introduction, telling the students what had happened to me and what the police had told me about the driver. They were quite quiet through this part, I paused for some questions but none was forthcoming so I moved quickly on to the extract from John Miller's investigation. The students really seemed to be interested in that. The fact that the two girls had also been sixth form students seemed to resonate with them. I was certain that even Grumpy Isaac couldn't have faulted the section that I'd selected. The students were a little more animated as I stopped the video, so I decided to capitalise and ask if any of them had any comments on what they'd just seen. They looked sideways at each other and a couple seemed to want to say something but they held back.

Grumpy Isaac jumped in, "Come on you lot. Surely one of you must have something you want to ask?" Somehow, I wasn't surprised that the students were reticent about speaking out in front of him, he was the sort to belittle any question, so I jumped in with a simple one of my own:

"The two girls were sixth form students, like yourselves. They were just 18, are any of you 18 yet?" I knew they weren't but it was a good start. One volunteered that she was the oldest in the class at 17 and another had only just had his sixteenth birthday at the end of the summer holidays. I carried on asking simple, fairly straightforward questions about what they'd just seen and then started to ask about their emotional reactions. I'd spent over 10 years as an auditor and one of the skills that had given me was the ability to get information from reluctant interviewees. I have to say that my accountancy training had been very good but I'd never envisaged that I would use it to encourage a group of teenagers to talk about drugs.

We were really getting into a good conversation when Grumpy Isaac interrupted to say that the hour was up and we should take a break. I got the distinct impression that he was ruffled because the session had gone so well and he hadn't been able to take charge. It was only a small victory for me but one I was well prepared to accept.

We had our tea and biscuit break and then started back but the momentum had been lost. Grumpy Isaac barked instructions at the students about how he wanted them to approach the task. I could see that the technicalities were disheartening them, and they soon went quiet again. When I got a chance, I started to ask about other campaigns that they'd seen. They were already warm to my questions and we got a debate going again. We looked at some different sorts of advertising and social media and started to put a plan together with the group splitting into different teams to tackle different areas. By the end of the second hour they had a plan to work on, roles were assigned and a timetable set. They had even adapted my phrase from the interview into a slogan: "Don't be an ass, don't be a mule!"

Normality

I was buzzing when I got back to the cabin. Even the weather had cheered up, well, at least it had stopped raining. I decided that, as I was on a high, I would go dancing tonight. My regular class was running a free-style evening and had offered me a free ticket. I had no excuse for not going and I'd promised Eddie that I would be there. I couldn't let her down.

I started to settle in to a routine over the next few days. On dry days, I carried on tidying up the site. I'd started to sort the debris into piles. A pile of broken rubbish for a skip, a pile of roof tiles, and piles of bricks, rubble, wood, textiles, plastics, glass, and anything else that might come in useful later. I ran out of space on the patio, so started on the lawn. It would ruin the grass but that could be re-turfed later. Anything that was remotely salvageable was stored in the garage or the chicken shed.

I took out windows, removed doors and pulled up floorboards. Then I took a sledgehammer to some of the loose brickwork, mentally placing a picture of Grumpy Isaac before I swung. The bricks flew out of the wall and I jumped back away from the flying debris. It was slightly scary just how easily the house could be demolished with muscle power and a sledgehammer.

Katherine the Surveyor visited on Monday to check on the damage. She explained that they hadn't used plasticiser in cement back in the 1930's so it was much more brittle than modern varieties. The impact of the lorry had probably sent shockwaves through the mortar holding the bricks together causing them to loosen. It didn't take much to take the house apart. I had a scaffolding tower that I'd bought when I was converting the flats and it was perfect for the job in hand.

But it was hard, physical work that I just wasn't used to. I'd spent my entire adult life sitting in front of a computer for 40 or 50 hours a week. My middle-aged joints soon started to protest and I began to look forward to wet days when I could stay inside, warmed by the newly installed log-burner. When I could research and design my new home or piece together the tattered bits of my old bed linen into patchwork curtains for the cabin using Rhona's sewing machine.

But at least I had a reason to delay job hunting.

There are many who are natural accountants, but I am not one of them. Although not ideal, my role at the electronics company had, at least, been varied. The European division made up about a third of the Group so we were a major part of their operation. The Group was growing rapidly and we acquired subsidiaries in the newly opened up Eastern European markets. I got to work on the acquisitions, which was, at the same time, exciting and tedious. Exciting as I got to travel around Europe and to the States on a regular basis. There were high-powered meetings with directors and financiers and, after a while, I was invited to attend shareholder events in New York. But the long hours, tough deadlines and, eventually, the repetition made it tedious. The Finance Director moved on and I was rewarded for my dedication and loyalty by being promoted into the role.

It was a big pay rise but, with it, came even longer hours and more stress.

One of the parts I really hated was lying to my colleagues and friends. The Group's shares were listed on the New York Stock Exchange, which imposed on us a raft of rules and regulations. In particular, any activity that might affect the share price, such as an acquisition, had to be declared to the shareholders at exactly the same time as it became known to the general public. That meant that all negotiations had to be carried out in utter secrecy. Whenever I was involved, I had to pretend to other people that there was nothing going on. Time after time, colleagues would ask me what was happening. I had to front it out, tell them nothing. I was only going on a routine visit to the Paris office, I wasn't really carrying out a due diligence exercise at a potential new acquisition in Brussels. I could just about justify the deceit, as it was a legal requirement of my role. The part I hated most was that I was getting quite good at it.

But a few months before the Brexit referendum, the American directors started to discuss the idea of moving the European Headquarters to Dublin. Jealous of the tax savings that the likes of Microsoft and Amazon were enjoying there, they'd started to investigate the benefits of moving to Ireland and being part of the Eurozone. They'd discovered that the lower cost of land and employment, together with the generous incentives that might be available from the Irish government as well as the tax benefits, would more that compensate for the cost of the move. The worst form of deceit was to work with my colleagues every day and not let on to them that their lives were about to be shattered.

The US team were clever operators. They waited until three months after the Brexit vote before announcing the move. That way, they could blame it on Brexit and not have to admit that it was purely profit driven. The staff who worked in the UK sales business would stay on in one floor of our existing offices reporting in to Dublin but all of the people who worked in the European management team would get a simple choice, move to Ireland or be made redundant. Most would choose to leave. I, along with over 80 people finished during the months following the announcement.

My boss, The European Chief Executive, promptly moved out to Dublin, with a generous relocation package, to set up the new office. I wasn't given the opportunity to go with him. Had I been, I doubt I would have accepted. Instead I stayed behind to wind up the old company, make the staff redundant and re-let the other two floors of the offices. It was the last straw in a career that I just about tolerated.

I was, at least, given a generous redundancy package and I'd planned to use it to change careers. Perhaps move into a role that made more use of my design skills. I wondered about doing a Masters degree and perused the courses available. The history of garden design was a possibility or a study of the influence of the Moors on European textiles. That one was in Barcelona.

In the end, I'd decided to take the time off until Christmas to decide what I wanted to do. If I hadn't had any inspiration by then, I would contract for a while. Maybe find a part-time contract doing something with no stress and regular hours? Or even do voluntary work. The National Trust were advertising for a volunteer to bake cakes in the café at their Swindon Head Office. That was appealing.

But now that inspiration had arrived. If I was careful with my finances I could live for a while on the income from the flats and my redundancy package. That would allow me to project manage the build of my new house full time. Perhaps I could persuade Kevin McCloud to film me doing it?

My life took on a new rhythm, there was Christmas shopping to be done, food to be bought, housework to do, Philpot and the chickens to be fed. I used to take my spare eggs to work but they started to stack up, so now I had to find a new market for them. I thought about catching the school-run parents with a stall outside the gate but, in the end, a quick trip around the neighbours and I had enough regular orders to take all the spares. Every delivery meant stopping for a chat which gave me a chance to get to know them better. There were Christmas parties at dancing and at football and I was even invited to the Christmas party with those who remained at the office – it was a bittersweet reunion. I looked after my nephews while Rosemary and Rob went to his office party and I chauffeured Alison and Barry to the Base's Christmas reunion.

Alan was a regular visitor to help me with large jobs and I helped him with the van. We stripped it down and built it back up, cleaning, repairing what could be repaired and replacing what couldn't. The van might have been free but the replacement parts cost me a couple of hundred quid. Alan, bless him, gave his time for free, but I could see that he got his own reward when, on the last possible day, it sailed through its MOT with just a minor advisory about the nearside brake pads.

It took a while to get used to the stove. I'd had a log fire in the house but that was more for effect than warmth and I only tended to light it on special occasions. This was different; suddenly the fire was a necessity. I learned how to light it and keep it going. I got into a routine of diving out of bed first thing, getting the fire going and then jumping back into the warmth of the duvet and going back to sleep while the cabin heated up. While Philpot learned to curl up in front of it, I learned to cook on it. I started with a camping kettle of water, worked up to soup, then stews. I developed a great recipe for rice pudding and even managed a three-ingredient fruitcake in a makeshift Dutch oven fashioned out of Gran's old roasting tin. I dried apple slices and made jams and chutneys from my garden produce. I was getting quite good at the "Good Life".

Doing lunch

Alan had said that the first few days of being home felt like being on holiday and I was beginning to understand what he meant. The first couple of weeks of not working had been an adventure and I'd been so busy that the days passed in a blur but, on the Monday before Christmas, I began to realise that this was a new normality. It was one of those cold but crisp winter days that just beckon you outdoors. It seemed such a shame to be inside but, quite frankly, I'd started to get a little bit bored with the jobs I had to do outside. Not that there wasn't plenty to do. There were still weeds to weed, fallen leaves to clear up and the green house could do with a clean. I'd made good inroads into demolishing the house but there was plenty more to pull down. The one thing I did know was that any of those chores would mean being on my own, again.

Working in an office means that you are always surrounded by people. I'd only ever worked in open-plan offices so, for at least eight hours a day, five days a week, there'd be conversation, chit chat, movement, and noise. For the last three weeks, I'd been on my own more than I'd been with others. I wasn't lonely as such, especially as my social life had improved now that I had more time, but I just suddenly found myself missing the company of others.

It occurred to me that I still had some present buying left to do. I always managed to get the Christmas presents sorted in time but I kept forgetting the two people with birthdays just after Christmas. One was my nephew and the other a good friend from football. I decided to head down to the Swindon Outlet Village to get those last two presents. Then I remembered that three of my former colleagues had found themselves new positions in the IT team at the Heelis building, the offices of the National Trust, next to the Outlet Village. Maybe I could kill two birds with one stone and see if they were free for lunch? I sent Harry a quick text message and started to get ready.

My phone buzzed, Harry had replied. I picked it up and saw the first line of the text, which made my heart sink. 'Sorry, team Xmas lunch today.' I pressed reply and was about to type something along the lines of, 'no worries, another time,' when I realised that the message continued: 'but Sarah and I finish at 4. Fancy a coffee and a cake?' That cheered me up. I decided to walk to get a different type of exercise. If I bought anything heavy, I could always get a bus home. Catching a bus was something I hadn't done in a long time.

I pottered around the Outlet Village but didn't find much inspiration so I decided to walk into the town centre. There's an underpass that takes foot traffic under the railway line and into the town. If only I could remember where it was. The whole area had changed a lot since I was last there. New flats and offices had been created from the old railway works, and I was confused about which way to go. I needn't have worried; there were lots of people walking towards me from the far corner of the square outside the Steam museum. I figured that they must have been returning to work from town and, if I walked against the flow of people, I'd find the underpass. I didn't pay any attention to the two men who were following me. I didn't even think anything was particularly unusual when, just as I turned the corner into the underpass, one of them caught up with me and grabbed my elbow saying, "Excuse me." I just assumed that I was about to be asked directions to somewhere. The security guard was in his wooden hut but he didn't look up.

But just at that point someone shouted, "Sam!" It was Harry who, with Sarah and Tim, was walking towards me through the underpass. They were on their way back from their Christmas lunch. The man who'd grabbed my elbow just muttered an apology and he and his mate walked on extremely quickly. That was odd, why didn't he ask whatever it was that he wanted? But I forgot the incident completely when the others caught up with me and we did the "How are you?" small talk. We agreed to meet up later in the café at Heelis, and I carried on into town. I didn't see the two strangers again but I did get the two presents I needed.

Christmas wishes

A lot of people have their Christmas traditions. Your parents one year, mine the next. Men to the pub while the women drink wine at home and complain about spending the entire morning cooking. Grandpa snoring through the Queen's speech while Auntie Edna gets merry on the sherry. But Christmas traditions weren't something that I'd ever really gone in for.

I can remember a couple of years of Christmas, early on at my grandparents' farm. Uncle Barry wasn't there as he was busy being the hero, saving his country on manoeuvres somewhere abroad. Dad, on the other hand, was branded unworthy by my grandmother because he chose to work on Christmas Eve at some event or grand party in London for double pay. He'd finally get home at 3 or 4 on Christmas morning, exhausted, and fit only to sleep for the rest of the day.

Planning wasn't one of Gran's top skills and poor Aunt Alison couldn't be expected to run around after the rest of us when she was trying to bring up two children with her husband on the other side of the world. So it fell to Mum to do all the shopping and preparation – after all, it was school holidays so she had nothing better to do.

But Christmas on a farm isn't the idyll of the TV turkey adverts. Cows still had to be brought in and milked, the pigs needed feeding and mucking out and Grandpa somehow managed to find chores that needed Dad's help, exhausted as he was.

After a while we stopped going to the farm for Christmas lunch, spending most of the day at home, just the three of us. Mum and I would go to bed early on Christmas Eve so that we could wake up when Dad got home. He'd dress up as Santa and arrive with a bag of presents that we'd open while munching on mince pies that Mum and I had made on Christmas Eve. The presents weren't fancy or expensive and tended towards things that were necessary rather than fun, but I never went without a toy, a game, or a book. We'd go back to bed, and I was under strict instructions not to get out again before midday so that Dad could sleep. I didn't mind, I had my book or my toy. In the afternoon, Mum and I would walk down to the farm for tea and cake and return home for turkey dinner later in the evening.

After Dad left, Mum and I returned to the farm for Christmas but life had changed. Alison, Sarah, and Alan would fly off to meet Barry for a holiday together so it was just my grandparents, Mum, and I. Gran had developed dementia by then so, once again, Mum ran the show. Then Grandpa had his heart attack in the field. He wasn't found until a neighbour saw Gran walking along the road in her nightdress and went to investigate. The farm was sold and Gran went into a home. We'd visit for an hour or so on Christmas Day to give her presents of underwear or stockings but she didn't recognise us.

Mum and I had several Christmases just for two and then she, too, was gone. After that it was E.J. and I. We had Christmases alone at home, Christmases on holiday, Christmases with friends but the two of us never had Christmas with our families.

Since E.J. left, I've been finding different ways to spend Christmas. A singles holiday (I was the youngest by 20 years), Christmases with Rosemary and my nephews, Christmas with Dad and Sandra (only once), Christmas with Sarah and her family, Christmas with Alan and Rhona before they left for Borneo. I spent one Christmas volunteering at a soup kitchen. Another was spent housesitting a Tudor Castle in Wales on my own, looking after the owners' 4 huskies and 3 Siamese cats while the owners spent Christmas in Turkey (as you do). That was probably my favourite year.

The decision was made for me this year. Alison was whisked into hospital the week before Christmas and it was touch and go whether she would be out before the big day. Neither Barry nor Alan knew their fan assisted from their combination ovens and I didn't think that they would manage to get turkey and all the trimmings on the table without a side order of food poisoning. So, when Alan asked if I wanted to stay with them over Christmas, I volunteered to earn my keep by doing the cooking.

They'd started packing for the move when I arrived on Christmas Eve with the food. I'd managed a surprising amount from the garden: butternut squash soup to start, potatoes, sprouts, and parsnips to accompany the turkey Barry had bought from the farm shop that had been set up in Grandpa's old tractor shed. I picked sage and pulled onions for the stuffing and got apples and pears out of the store in the garage to go with the cheese course. I'd made mincemeat from apples, quinces and berries for my own "quincemeat" pies and dried apples, blueberries and currants went into the pudding. I was pretty proud of myself.

We had a quiet Christmas Day. Alison was just out of hospital and extremely weak and tired. Dinner courses were taken slowly and spread out so she could rest with Barry by her side. To give them space, Alan and I started packing up the spare room.

"How's she doing really?" I asked him.

"It's tough. She's really worried after what happened to your Mum."

"That was a long time ago. Medicine has come a long way since then. You said they caught it early."

"Yeah, they think so. I just can't imagine life without her. I don't know how you managed all those years. All this makes me realise, we should have been there, you know, done more to help."

I was stunned. Alison and Alan had been my life support during Mum's illness. Alan had been round every other day to help with odd jobs. He'd helped me to decorate the dining room and move Mum's bed in there when she couldn't get upstairs. Alison had shopped, cooked, cleaned and sat with Mum while I studied or worked. Even Sarah had popped in when she could but it was a long journey, from her home in Bracknell, with the twins.

"You and Alison were fabulous. You couldn't have done more. I'd never have coped with out you." He looked at me and I could see that his eyes were red. I gave him a bear hug. "She'll be good, you'll see! Now give me a hand with these blankets, let's use them to wrap those pictures."

Hidden in plain sight

I stayed another night but needed to get back for Philpot and the chickens on Boxing Day. I loaded my car with firewood from their shed, it'd been a long time since they'd had a log fire and there wasn't even a fireplace at their new house. The weight of the wood was putting pressure on the axles so I had to drive slowly, much to the annoyance of Black Leathers on the Ducati that insisted on following me back to Swindon. As we came past the village of Vastern, I slowed and indicated for her to overtake but I noticed her waiting on Royal Wootton Bassett High Street and suddenly she was behind me again. I began to feel uncomfortable about her knowing where Alan and his family lived.

She shot ahead of me when I got to the Great Western Way, and I lost sight of her. I hoped that she'd worked out that I was just going home and had given up. But when I got back to the cabin I guessed that the reason she'd shot off had been to warn whoever had been at the cabin that I was on my way back. I'd been broken into again. They were certainly determined to get the SD card back. This time they'd broken a window to get in. It had obviously only just happened, as the rain hadn't yet dampened the carpet. I fetched a piece of spare board from the garage and fixed it over the window.

I went in search of Philpot. He had a clockwork pet feeder that I used if I was going away for the weekend. I could fill it with enough food for two days and the cover slowly opened to reveal the food – keeping it fresh. In the house, Philpot had used a cat flap and could come and go as he pleased but I hadn't fitted one in the cabin as it would be too draughty. That had given me a dilemma for Christmas. I didn't want to leave Philpot locked inside the cabin for two days while I was away but I didn't want to leave his food outside where it would be eaten by the local rats and foxes.

Instead, I'd fitted a cat flap into the hen house and put Philpot's food, water, and a brand-new cat bed on the floor under the chickens' shelf. Effectively I'd created an apartment block for the pets. Philpot had the downstairs apartment, and the chickens had the upstairs. As I walked across to the hen house, I saw Philpot coming out licking his lips. I hoped that it was cat food that he'd found palatable and that he hadn't found a way of getting to the chickens. But I needn't have worried. It seemed that the new neighbours had got on well. The cat food had been eaten, the bed had been slept in, and there were half a dozen eggs waiting for me in the nesting box.

I decided that I needed to do something about the SD card. They'd failed to find it so far. The first time, it had been in my jeans pocket. This time, it was hidden in the secret drawer in the linen press. But what about next time? And the time after? I had to make my mind up about the money. Would I retrieve it? The drugs dealers clearly hadn't been able to or they wouldn't have searched the cabin again. How did they know I had the SD card? Had they seen me pick it up? Otherwise, surely, they would assume the police had it. Perhaps they had 'someone on the inside' who told them that the SOCO team hadn't found it. If the money wasn't collected by the 30th it would be returned to the sender and then it would be too late. Too late for me, as well, if I wanted it for myself. I reasoned that I had a right to it. OK, I was insured but I would only get the house rebuilt and new things bought. I wouldn't get my precious photographs back and my college portfolio was lost forever. I wouldn't get any compensation for the stress I'd suffered (hmm, there wasn't a lot of that to be honest) but I had spent a lot of my time sorting out stuff. I had talked myself into keeping it when I started to think about the practicality and the legality (or not). If I did get it, what would I do with it? I knew that I couldn't bank it. The banks ask questions if you try to bank more than a tenner in cash these days, so quite how would I explain quarter of a million? If I kept it as cash, where would I keep it? Whoever it was that had searched the cabin twice weren't going to stop. They'd keep coming back until they found the money. Perhaps I should hand the card in to the police after all. Tell them that I'd just found it. I was back to indecision.

Whatever I decided, I still felt that I needed to get rid of the SD card. I fired up the netbook and checked the photos again. I only needed the code, the rest I could remember. How could I record the code so it wouldn't be obvious? I thought about just writing it on a post-it note on the fridge. After all – nobody would know what it was, but then a better idea came to me.

I flicked through my notebook. It was my overflow memory and I used it to store all sorts of information. I listed websites and names of tradespeople, I kept recipes and shopping lists, notes of conversations and, more recently, the weekend before the lorry crash, I had written some measurements in it for some shelves that I'd started to fit in the spare bedroom. I'd left the notebook in the workshop so it had survived the house collapsing.

Near the front, I came across some notes I'd made a year or so earlier when I'd been organising a weekend away for a group of friends. We were now spread around the country so were all going to meet up in London and I'd had a discount voucher for train tickets. I'd booked all the tickets and written down the booking codes in the notebook against the names of all my friends except Max and Mina who were making their own way from Manhattan. There was a space next to their names in my list. I realised that the security code for the DirectDeliver locker was the same number of seemingly random digits as the booking code for the train journeys. I grabbed a pen and wrote the number in against the entry for Max and Mina. Then I wiped the card. If the drugs dealers (or the police) found it now, it wouldn't be much use to them.

I tidied up the mess from the break-in and swept up the glass. Once again, they hadn't taken anything, so, once again, I didn't bother reporting it to the police. I unloaded the logs from the car into the log store, had a light supper and settled down to a batch of Christmas specials on DVD that I'd brought back from Alison's.

Kidnapped

I'd been looking forward to the day after Boxing Day. It was a day I traditionally spent with Rosemary and the boys.

I'd been furious when, seven months after splitting from Mum, Dad told me I had a half sister. She was a healthy, full-term baby and, even as a 10 year old, I knew what that meant.

Sandra, my stepmother, had a jealous, possessive streak and put obstacles in the way of Dad seeing me. She didn't like the fact that her new husband had a past. We'd tried my staying over with them at weekends but, somehow, she managed to make me feel very unwelcome. Mum didn't take much persuading that it wasn't working. Sandra didn't like Dad spending the day with me instead of her but we eventually found a compromise. Sandra could just about cope with Dad going to football matches and he was allowed a season ticket to Swindon Town's home matches. What he didn't tell her was that he'd bought me one as a Christmas present and we got together at every home match. There was usually a minibus going to the game from Lyneham so Dad and I met at the kebab van in the car park at the County Ground. We'd watch the game together and then he'd take me for a pie and a pint of fizzy pop at one of the pubs in Old Town before running me home. Sandra was just grateful that, even though Dad went for a drink with his 'mates' after the game, he didn't come home drunk.

But this time Dad came to our house to see me. When he told me that I had a little sister, I was upset. It wasn't that I didn't want a sibling, it was just that the timing proved that Dad had been cheating on Mum which upset me. I lashed out at him, thumping him hard in the chest.

Mum was the peacemaker. She held me and cuddled me and let me cry and then she explained that she wasn't angry. Their relationship had been over when Dad had met Sandra. She was pleased that Dad had met someone who made him happy and she was delighted that I had a little sister. Then she told me that she, too, had news, she'd been seeing someone else for a few weeks, a groundsman at the base called, Alex, and she hoped that I'd like to meet him.

I never did meet Alex but I did forgive Dad. He took me back to meet baby Rosemary and let me hold her while Sandra fussed around as if I was going to break her precious china ornament. Motherhood mellowed Sandra and she made more of an effort to welcome me into their family but I didn't really get to know Rosemary until she was about 14 and I was in my mid twenties.

Dad and Sandra went skiing every year. They'd taken Rosemary at first but she decided she hated it and, by the time she was a teenager, refused to go with them. For a couple of years, she simply stayed with Sandra's brother and his family for the week but, this particular year, there was a problem at the last minute and Rosemary couldn't stay at her uncle's. I'd got the week booked off work to study for my first accountancy exams and Dad, upon hearing this, pressed me to baby-sit Rosemary. At first it had been awkward, we barely knew each other and there I was staying in her home, telling her to get ready for school. But, on the Monday evening,

I took her to a pub nearby for dinner and let her stay up too late for a school night and she quickly decided I was cool.

Rosemary loved cooking and, for the rest of the week, I'd pick her up from school and we'd prepare a meal together. Mum had always done the cooking at home so I hadn't done much more than simple meals but Rosemary's interest in different foods was infectious and I'd come away from that week much more interested in cooking.

Rosemary was grown up now, married with two boys, Toby and Oliver, my nephews. They were now of an age where they were great fun and Rosemary would let them stay with me from time to time. We climbed trees and caught bugs and made mud-pies together and Dad and I taught them the importance of football.

My indecision about the SD card would have to stretch for yet another day. Someone called Wendy Holmes in Cheltenham had offered me some furniture and I was due to look at it in the morning. I would take the van up to Cheltenham, collect the furniture and then off to Rosemary's for Toby's party in the afternoon. With Toby's birthday being so close to Christmas, Rosemary tried to make it a special day for him. So many people with birthdays at that time of year lose out because of the overwhelming concentration on Christmas but Rosemary was determined that her son wouldn't be one of them.

I set off for Cheltenham earlier than I needed to. Alan had warned me that the van's brakes still weren't yet as good as they could be. The new brake pads hadn't arrived and the van was pulling to the right when the brakes were applied, so I should take it easy and not try to stop suddenly. It was the first time I'd driven the van any distance on my own and I was getting used to it as I travelled along Gloucester Road so I barely noticed the Ducati pulling out behind me near the junction with Cirencester Way.

It was only when we got onto the dual carriageway that I realised that, once again, Black Leathers was following me. How did she know I would be heading out? Was she waiting somewhere, spying on me all the time as I moved around the cabin and the garden? I was more annoyed that scared. What could they do? I'd be safe enough in the van. Would they try something while I was collecting the furniture? I'd Googled the house I was going to. It was an ordinary house on an ordinary residential street. There'd be people around. Wendy Holmes had said that her brother would be there to help load the van. Whoever my stalker was, they wouldn't risk trying anything in front of strangers, would they?

I deliberately took it gently, even more gently that I really needed to. I was hoping that Black Leathers would get bored following me and give up, there was no way I could outrun her in the van.

There was a surprising amount of traffic on the A417 for a weekday morning in the holidays. Clearly a lot of people were returning home after Christmas. Cars of families loaded up with their Christmas presents finally getting away from the in-laws. There were a lot of lorries too. It was the day the stores switched their stock from pre-Christmas to New Year's sales and goods were being moved around the country.

As always, we crawled through the single lane section at Nettleton Bottom, past the Golden Heart pub. E.J. loved the Cotswolds and we'd often walked or brought the bikes to cycle around this part of Gloucestershire, stopping at the Golden Heart or one of the other lovely country pubs in the area.

At the top of the hill, after the village, the traffic eased along the ridge and we got a little speed up but this was a road I'd travelled before and I knew that we'd slow down again as we headed back down towards the Air Balloon roundabout. I allowed the car in front of me to pull ahead; I'd catch him up soon enough. Just as we came over the brow of the hill, before we reached the entrance to the pub car park, I suddenly became aware of something coming up on my outside. A glance in my wing-mirror showed me Black Leathers was overtaking. I just had time to think, "thank goodness – she's getting fed up and going", when she slewed across in front of me.

My instinct was to jam my brakes on and steer to the left to avoid her and the traffic coming in the other direction, but the van had other ideas. The driver's side front brake bit fractionally faster than it's counterpart and the van pulled back to the right. The van wobbled ominously for a second or two before coming to a stop in the middle of the road. I couldn't help thinking that, had the brakes not been faulty, the whole van would have spun around to the left and toppled over. I'd been foolish to brake so hard and swerve. It might have been the right course of action in my car but not in such a big vehicle. Ironically, the faulty brakes had saved me. I looked back and saw that Black Leathers hadn't been so lucky. She'd come off the bike a few yards back and was lying in the road.

Dumping the van into the pub car park, I ran back. I had my mobile phone in my hand to call the emergency services, but an ambulance shot out of the car park and was on the scene in an instant. It was handy that an ambulance would be waiting right at the scene of the accident. But the Air Balloon junction and Crickley Hill were accident black spots and there were often ambulances waiting in that area. As I got close, a small knot of people had formed around the bike and rider but I seemed to get propelled to the front, almost as if someone had parted the onlookers. One of the ambulance crew pulled a wallet out of the rider's pocket and pulled out a credit card.

"Wendy Holmes" he read off the card. It was odd but he almost seemed disappointed as he said it.

"Wendy!" I repeated involuntarily. I leant forward to look at my stalker. My heart stopped. This was the Wendy Holmes I was going to meet. She'd arranged a trap. She was luring me to the house in Cheltenham to, what? Get me to tell her where the money was? What was she going to do? Get her brother (was there really a brother?) to tie me up and torture me.

"You know her," someone said. It was more of a statement than a question. "You'd better go with her." Before I could protest I was bundled into the ambulance with her and the doors were slammed shut. I started to say that I didn't know her but it occurred to me that I really ought to tell the police about this. She was clearly part of the drugs gang that had lured Markus Stalbrigg into taking the fatal decision to swallow the bags of heroine. I could call Detective Keith from the ambulance; get him to meet us at the hospital.

I was sat in the back of the ambulance with one of the paramedics while the other was driving. The one in the back was fussing around Wendy, trying to take her pulse and blood pressure. She appeared to be unconscious and he was trying hard to bring her round. It occurred to me that it had all happened very fast. It wasn't like this on TV. On Casualty, they'd have assessed her first before setting off, probably set up an I.V. line, monitored her U's and E's and done something with her FBC's. But this crew had just bundled her, and me, straight into the ambulance, and set off. She wasn't even strapped onto the trolley. The paramedic in the back was trying to do that as we turned the corner to head down Crickley Hill. As we took the sharp bend, Wendy started to slide off the trolley. I stood up and placed my weight against her body so that the paramedic could get the strap around her. I noticed that he was fumbling and that he looked surprisingly scared.

"I'm Sam." I volunteered.

"Hi Sam, I'm Niall." He replied. "Would you mind just pulling that strap over, need to get her properly secured there" he continued.

"We set off in rather a hurry, didn't we?"

"We need to get her to hospital as quickly as we can." He replied. "Nasty things motorbike accidents. She's unconscious and not coming round. We need to get her a brain scan as quickly as we can to see what's going on."

I pulled my phone out of my pocket. "Which hospital are we going to?" I needed to tell Detective Keith where we were headed.

"You can't use that in here. It interferes with the equipment."

"Oh!" I started to put my phone away but something was niggling me. Hadn't they announced on the news a year or so ago that they'd worked out it wasn't true. Mobile phone signals didn't impact on medical equipment at all. They were always using them on Casualty.

I glanced through to the front of the ambulance. We were still on the dual carriageway. We'd passed the turning into Cheltenham, which made me uneasy, but I had a feeling that Cheltenham hospital didn't have full A&E facilities. I tried again.

"Are we going to Gloucester?"

Niall shouted to the driver "Where are we going Jimmy?"

"Southmead" came the reply. Bristol! I hadn't counted on going all the way to Bristol.

"No, I can't." I started to protest. "The van... I have an appointment." How was I going to get back in time to collect the van and get to Stroud for Toby's party?

The more I thought about it, the more I knew something wasn't right. It'd been too easy for me to get through the knot of people around Wendy at the accident. Someone had helped me, moved people out of the way. The same person who'd shouted, "You know her. You'd better go with her" and propelled me into the ambulance. I could feel my adrenaline rising. I had fast tracked beyond worrying and achieved panicking very quickly. That wouldn't help at all. I needed to keep a clear head.

I'd sat with Mum through several sessions with the Macmillan nurses as they helped her to manage her pain and stress levels. I'd been by her side as we practiced breathing and distraction techniques together. Those techniques had been helpful in my subsequent career. Being a Chartered Accountant, with tight deadlines and large budgets at stake can be pretty stressful. I concentrated on my breathing and used small, controlled physical actions, stretching, scratching my head and arching my back, to distract from the stress and panic. It worked.

Niall was fussing more now. "She's not right." He shouted to Jimmy. "She's in a bad way. We need to stop and assess her. I've got to stabilise her. I can't do that while we're moving."

"We can't stop." Came the reply. "You know what'll happen if we do." I raised an eyebrow. My non-verbal communication detector was working overtime. Niall was panicking. Jimmy was panicking. I was trying my hardest to stop panicking. I looked straight at Niall and asked, "What will happen if we stop?"

He looked at me as if he was about to speak but just then Wendy made a choking sound and her head started to jerk.

"She's having a seizure!" Shouted Niall. "We've got to stop, Jimmy. This wasn't in the plan."

If I'd had a sense that something wasn't quite right, now I convinced of it. I joined in, "Yes, Jimmy, Wendy wasn't supposed to get hurt was she? I'm the one who should be strapped to the trolley."

Niall looked up at me, shocked. "You know?"

I raised an eyebrow. "I do now."

Wendy jerked again. Niall looked back at her. "Her breathing's weak, we need to stop! Now!"

"Stop! Now!" I echoed. Jimmy sighed. We were on the M5, heading south towards Bristol. He pulled the ambulance to a halt on the hard shoulder and climbed through into the rear. I swapped places with him to make space for the two of them to work. While they were pre-occupied with trying to resuscitate Wendy, I called Detective Keith.

"Sam – what do you want?" He was clearly irritated. It was the day after Boxing Day after all. He was probably at home, on leave. I glanced back to where the paramedics were desperately trying to revive a very limp Wendy. "I've been kidnapped." I said "And I think my stalker's about to die."

Rescue

I could almost hear Detective Keith jump to his feet, the irritation in his voice gone. "What's happening? Where are you? Are you OK?" He quizzed. I told him about the bike, the accident and the ambulance.

"Do you know where you are?" He asked. I looked out of the windscreen.

"Yes, I'm exactly a mile north of junction 12 on the hard shoulder of the M5 southbound." I replied.

"Exactly a mile north." He repeated.

"Yes," I replied, "exactly". I glanced again at the road sign immediately in front of the ambulance. A mile, that's definitely what it said.

"Stay where you are, I'll get some uniformed officers to you as quickly as I can." He rang off.

The two paramedics were sitting now, heads bowed, hands in their laps. I looked at Niall and raised an eyebrow. "She's dead." He said simply. I felt as if someone had poured cold gravy down my insides. I shook my head. "I assume that wasn't supposed to happen?" I was looking at Jimmy this time. Even with his head bowed, I could see that his skin had turned grey and his dreadlocks were shaking. "I suggest you tell me what was supposed to happen."

It was Niall who answered. "Nobody was supposed to die. We were supposed to take you to a house in Bristol and hand you over. They've got his brother." He nodded his head towards Jimmy who was still shaking.

I raised the other eyebrow. Niall continued. "Jimmy's brother's a smack head. He owes money to his dealer. This morning, when we arrived at the station, some low-life was waiting for Jimmy. They showed him a picture of his brother tied to a chair. If we didn't do what they asked, they would kill him."

This time I raised both eyebrows. "We were to wait at the Air Balloon car park. There would be an accident. Initially we were told it would be a BMW," (I drive a BMW) "but then we got a phone call to say it would be a red van". We were to grab the driver, tell everyone you were concussed and we were taking you to hospital. Instead we were to take you to the house in Bristol where we'd hand you over and get Charlie back. They promised they wouldn't hurt you. They just wanted some information."

"They'll kill him!" Jimmy whispered.

The cold gravy inside me congealed. Taking that SD card had put Jimmy's brother's life at risk and had caused Wendy's death. But I still couldn't understand how they knew I had it. They couldn't have seen me pick it up, even PC William hadn't seen me pick it up and he'd been right next to me.

I could hear sirens and, in a few seconds, a police car had pulled in behind the ambulance. The occupants waited, probably not sure what they were dealing with.

"Stay here!" I ordered the two paramedics. "I'll speak to them, tell them that you're not in this by choice."

I climbed out of the passenger door and walked towards the police car, my hands out by my sides where they could see them. I wasn't quite ready to put my arms in the air as they do in the films. The two police officers got out of the car. Another car, a motorway patrol, pulled in front of the ambulance. Traffic whisked past us on the motorway. As soon as I was close enough for them to hear I shouted: "I'm Sam Wilston. I'm the one who was kidnapped." I got close enough to explain that there were two genuine paramedics and a dead drug dealer inside. I hadn't seen any weapons. The paramedics weren't willing kidnappers; they'd been forced into it.

Party pooper

I met Detective Keith at Stroud police station. He held me there for over five hours going over the events. I told him about being followed home from Lyneham by Black Leathers, now known as Wendy. He asked why I hadn't reported it and I said that I hadn't realised it was significant until today. I told him about the second break-in. I wasn't even sure there had been a first so I didn't mention it. He asked why I hadn't reported that either, but I just said that I thought it was vandals and nothing had been taken.

I told him about being lured to Cheltenham and about the accident and repeated what Niall and Jimmy had said.

He asked me over and over what they were looking for. I had prepared for this question during my ride to Stroud in the back of the police car. In drama lessons at school we'd put on a play in which I'd acted the part of a prisoner of war who'd been questioned by the Nazis. We'd researched techniques that prisoners had used to avoid giving answers to questions. It was important to them to be able to say that they didn't know anything in a way that would make the interrogator believe them. I'd read that if you were lying you looked upwards and to the right so, in the police car, I had practiced avoiding do this. As soon as Detective Keith started to ask, "what do you think they were looking for?" I shut my eyes, put my forehead into my hands and rubbed my temples.

Then I held my hands out, eyes still shut, in a sign of despair before looking up at him.

"I've no idea." I looked him straight in the eye as I said this. "The paramedic said that I had information that Wendy wanted but I've been wracking my brains trying to think what that might be." I paused but Detective Keith didn't say anything. He was waiting for me to slip up, admit to something. I played along.

"I assume it'd be something drugs related but why do they think I'd have it? I scratched my head as I looked at him. "Your guys had the lorry. Surely if there was a parcel of drugs, it would be in the lorry. Why would they think that I had it?"

"You didn't go over to the lorry after the crash? Take something out of it?" Detective Keith was clearly suspicious but I didn't rise to the bait. I rested my chin on my hand while I pretended to think. The activity helped me to calm my breathing down so I didn't appear nervous. I shook my head, my chin still in my hand.

"No, I didn't get out of my car between calling 999 and PC William finding me. I was on the phone all that time."

Detective Keith nodded, "We listened to the recording of the call. You sounded very calm." It was almost an accusation. Did he think I'd orchestrated the accident?

I laughed. "Calm until I broke down. PC William thought I was in shock. He was taking my pulse and checking my breathing when I first registered he was there."

Detective Keith relaxed. "You didn't go back to the house after that?"

"Not until I saw you the next day and then PC William was with me all the time until I left with the surveyor."

We went back over the events of the lorry crash. He asked again about seeing the bike the following day. I told him again about the bike, about Wendy following me and about the break in on Boxing Day.

Detective Keith wanted to send some SOCOs round to look for evidence in the cabin. Fortunately, I didn't have to pretend to be calm at the suggestion as my stomach suddenly rumbled and we were both distracted. I apologised and he suggested that we take a break. I could get a sandwich from the canteen and he had some things to check up on. Perfect timing, I needed to work out how to hide that SD card before the SOCOs turned up. If they found it wiped but could, somehow, trace it back to Stalbrigg, they'd know I was planning to take the money.

When we got back together Detective Keith had some news. "Wendy Holmes was actually Wendy Watson." Well that was an ironic alias. "She's the daughter of Josh Watson. He's well known to the police all over the South West as being connected to the drugs trade but we've never had enough to charge him. His daughter's death, however, is a game changer. The Bristol police are talking to him now." They didn't waste their time.

"Oh and Jimmy the Paramedic's brother? Released unharmed by the drugs dealers." That was a relief.

"What'll happen to Jimmy and Niall?"

"I really wish I could say that no further action would be taken but it's out of my hands. The kidnapping happened on Gloucester police's patch, so I don't have jurisdiction. But it would help if you were to say that you weren't going to make a complaint against them."

I confirmed that I wouldn't.

The birthday party was long over. I'd managed to ring Rosemary on the way to the police station to warn her that I might not make it. It was her husband, Rob, who picked me up from the police station and took me to collect the van.

"I'm sorry for missing Toby's party." I started. "What did you tell him?"

"We told him what you said." Rob replied. I'd told Rosemary that I'd witnessed a fatal car accident and that I was going to the police station to give a witness statement. It wasn't a complete lie.

"Took a long time to give a witness statement." He commented.

"There was more to it." That wasn't a lie either. "I knew the person who died, well sort of. I hadn't actually met her before but when I saw her on the side of the road, I recognised her. She's been hanging around outside my house. I went in the ambulance so that I could tell the police that she'd been following me. The police think there's a drugs link to the crash at my house and it turns out she is... or, rather, she was, the daughter of a known drugs dealer. The police think that the drugs dealers are looking for something that might have been left at my house when the lorry crashed. We were going over and over what that might have been."

I didn't mention the break-ins or being followed the previous day. Rosemary, in particular, would worry. She might have insisted that I stayed with them but that might put her and the boys at risk.

I changed the subject. "How did the party go?"

Rob snorted. "Eight, six year old boys all hyper on Christmas sweets and treats. It was mayhem. I wish I'd had an excuse as good as yours to get out of it." We both laughed.

"Rosie asks if you want to come back to ours for tea? There's plenty of food left over."

The sandwich at the police station hadn't really filled the hole in my stomach but I was too tired and rattled to be sociable, especially with the boys who would have asked too many questions.

"Do you mind if I don't? I'm sorry but I'm knackered."

"That's what she said you'd say. She's packed a bag of party food for you in the back." It was scary that, even though I hadn't grown up with my younger sister, she knew me so well.

I gave Rob my present for Toby. "Can you give him this with my apologies. I'll pop over later in the week if you're going to be around?"

"Rosie'll be home with the boys tomorrow. I've got to work. We're off to my parents the next day for New Year."

Rob inspected the van when we got to the Air Balloon and pronounced it "Very practical." I didn't tell him that it had saved me from serious harm. "Do you think your cousin'd look at Rosie's hatchback? It's making an odd noise?" I said I'd ask and then climbed into the van to head for home.

Detective Keith had decided that it wasn't worth sending the SOCO team out now that they had Watson in for questioning. The SOCO team were short handed during the Christmas break and he wanted them at Watson's house first. As I expected, even when I had eventually reported the break-in, the police weren't interested in doing anything about it.

Decision

I hadn't fancied being sociable with Rosemary and her family but I wasn't sure I wanted to be on my own just yet either. The netbook that I had been using was old and slow with a dodgy screen. The first instalment of the insurance money had landed in my bank account so it was time to treat myself to a new computer. I'd planned to look online but what I really needed, I realised, was some advice from a 16 year old about the latest tech, so I headed to the Greenbridge Retail Park. Going to Greenbridge meant carrying on down the A419 to the Oxford Road junction. That meant going past Sainsbury's. That started me thinking again about the money sitting there.

The 16 year old talked me into a tablet with detachable keyboard. It'd be faster than the netbook and had a 4G connection. As my superfast cable broadband had been disrupted by the crash, I had been tethering the netbook to my phone but the connection was incredibly slow.

Computer shopping had cheered me up and, when I got back to the cabin, I fed Philpot, lit the fire, put my feet up, and consigned the netbook to a box in the henhouse. I'd just started to set up the new tablet when Detective Keith rang.

"We know now what they've been looking for. Watson was so distraught over his daughter that he spilled the whole plan." This was it; I'd have to admit to having the SD card. "Stalbrigg was an agency driver for a number of companies. As well as bringing in drugs from France, he was supposed to be bringing some money from drug dealers there who wanted to set up a supply line into Bristol and the West Country. The money was to buy their way into Watson's existing business. Stalbrigg dropped the money off at a safe house in Swindon and was heading up to North Swindon, near where Wendy Watson lived, with the details of where he'd left the cash. He never made it."

"Oh, so where did he leave the cash?" I asked, trying to just sound mildly curious.

"Watson didn't know. Stalbrigg had the details with him. He was going to drop them off for Wendy to pick up."

"So they must think that I know where it is." I mused out loud. "Why do they think I have the details, surely the SOCO team would have them?" I repeated my question from yesterday.

"Watson has a cousin who works in the forensics office as a cleaner. He's been through the evidence lists and the boxes and knows that there's nothing there. Therefore, they assume that you must have it."

"What about the dealers who sent the money? They must have known the plan?"

"Apparently not. Only Stalbrigg knew the exact details. As a driver going backwards and forwards from Britain to the continent all the time, he could set this up himself. The fewer people who knew the details, the better."

"Is that it over now?" I asked. "Now he's confessed, and she's dead, I assume they won't be coming after me again."

"Don't be so certain. We'll have to release Watson out on bail in the next day or so. Be vigilant and call if you see anything suspicious."

It also explained why Stalbrigg had been travelling the way he'd been going. He was an agency driver so, presumably, had worked for DirectDeliver at some point. He knew the procedure and the codes necessary for delivering a parcel into a DirectDeliver locker. He'd stashed the money, taken a picture of the parcel and the label and was heading towards the drop-off point to hand over the SD card. Wendy would then go to pick up the money. I remembered that her Ducati had panniers big enough to hold a substantial package of cash.

I had all the information I needed. I was the only one who knew where the money was. I'd had my house and all my personal things destroyed. I'd been broken into, stalked, followed (that was, kind of, the same thing), kidnapped and, worst of all, I'd missed my nephew's birthday party. I started to plan. I was due at Rosemary's for lunch the next day but I couldn't go empty handed. I needed to do some shopping on the way there.

I dressed carefully the following morning. In one of my earlier shopping trips, I'd bought myself a reversible hoodie. Being quite short on storage space, clothes that would do twice the work for half the cupboard space were a bonus. I wrote my shopping list in my notebook and then headed up to the garage for a box. I found just the thing. I'd ordered some boots off Ebay, and they'd arrived in a plain brown cardboard box. It was just the right size. Of course I'd hoarded the box, it was bound to come in useful at some point.

Gran's sister, Millie, was still alive and living in a care home on the outskirts of Bristol. I tried to visit her at least once a year and take her a hamper of homegrown food. I'd missed going this autumn because of the pressures of work so, to make up for it, I filled the box with treats. Some left over quincemeat pies, some of the better apples and pears that I was storing in the garage, a couple of jars of home made jam, and a jar of courgette chutney. I popped a Happy New Year card in and wrote in it that I would see her as soon as I could. Then I headed off to Sainsbury's.

Once again, my stress management techniques helped me to cope. I wasn't sure if it was stress, fear, or excitement or, probably, all three, but as I headed towards the DirectDeliver lockers, my stomach was definitely in knots. I'd made elaborate plans to give myself an alibi (if that was the right word). I would use the DirectDeliver system to send the parcel to Millie. If the police spotted me or saw me on CCTV or tracked me down any other way, I would have a legitimate reason to be there. I'd deliberately used a box that was roughly the same shape and size as the one I was collecting so that, again, if I was spotted, I could point to Millie's box and say that was the one they'd seen.

Then, wearing my hoodie inside out, I would collect the box of money and send it straight on to another DirectDeliver facility. That would give me another month to work out what to do. The plan was hideously complicated but I didn't trust anyone at that point. Not the police, the drugs dealers or, even, myself. I was trying to cover every eventuality that I could think of. I kept going over the steps in my head as I walked, pretending confidence, to the facility.

Sainsbury's was busy but the lockers were out of the way to one side of the entrance. There wasn't anyone else in that area. I put my box down at the desk and then, pretending to stretch my back out, looked around for cameras. I noticed one straight ahead at the check-in desk and one up to the right that would catch the faces of people as they walked up to the desk. I made a point of reading the instructions thoroughly. I put my box on the scales and entered the delivery details into the keypad. This box was going direct to Millie at the home.

I put the fee on my credit card and a sticker was printed which I fixed to the box. Then a locker clicked open and I put Millie's box inside. That was it done.

I nipped into Sainsbury's and picked up a few snacks and some indoor sparklers to take to Rosemary's, paying with a twenty-pound note, then headed back to the car. But I didn't drive away. Instead I swapped my hoodie inside out and wrapped an old Swindon Town football scarf around my mouth and nose. Then I headed back to the DirectDeliver lockers. I'd memorised the code so that I didn't need to get the notebook out of my pocket.

When I got to the desk, I took care not to look in the direction of the cameras. I punched the code into the keypad, which opened a locker to the right of the desk. I didn't need to worry about my fingerprints on the keypad as I'd already established a legitimate reason why they'd be there, but I put my thick woollen gloves back on to handle the box. Without even opening it, I put it back into the system. This time I addressed it to a DirectDeliver facility in Stroud. I was sure to have a legitimate reason to be visiting Stroud again in the near future and could collect it easily. In a perverse form of rebellion, I addressed it to Wendy Watson and put Josh Watson's name as the sender. It didn't matter as only I would see the box, but it did mean that, if the police intercepted it, it couldn't be traced back to me.

It was going to cost me a twenty but it was worth the investment. I paid cash into the machine. The twenty-pound note would also have my fingerprints on but, I reasoned, I would simply claim that it must be the same one that I'd paid for my shopping with. Someone else must have received it in change and used it to pay for their delivery.

I left and headed up to Stroud for a belated birthday party.

New Year's celebrations

I'd planned to go to the New Year's Eve dance this year as I did most years. Even if I didn't go to lessons much any more, the dances were worth going to. But the day was bright and not too cold, and I was itching to spend it in the garden. I'd have plenty of time to come in when it got dark, shower, change into my fancy dress costume, eat and go. I prepared a lamb casserole and popped it in the slow cooker that Sarah had given me for Christmas.

After weeding and digging the vegetable garden for four or five hours, my back was aching. Not the best idea if I was going dancing later. Mid afternoon, I went into the cabin for a loo break, a cup of tea, and an ibuprofen. I normally kept my phone in my back jeans pocket when I'm in the garden but I got it out to check for messages and then chucked it on the side while I made my tea. I didn't want to stay inside too long with the days being so short, so I took my tea and headed straight back out. I had one thing left to do in the daylight and that was to clean out the hen house.

Lying on the ground by the hen house door was the pink garden claw, sharpened prongs uppermost. I made a mental note to pick that up before I finished. It was a health and safety nightmare lying there like that. What if someone fell on it?

When I first got my chickens, I found their smell unpleasant and the idea of cleaning out the muck and used bedding from the hen house made me heave. But five years later and I was used to it. Especially in the cold weather, it didn't smell too bad. For a gardener, chicken muck is gold dust. It's full of nitrogen, which is great to help plants build healthy roots and leaves. I scraped out the old bedding into a large bucket and deposited it in the raised bed closest to the hen house door. By spring it would have broken down into lovely, rich compost. The soil in this part of Swindon is heavy clay mixed with the soft Cotswold gravel, which is mined in the gravel pits of the Cotswold Water Park only a few miles away. It makes the soil hard and high in lime which isn't great for growing much so I built raised beds in the kitchen garden edged with scaffolding planks and filled them each year with plenty of compost that I make myself in three big bays made out of old pallets. It had rained hard over the last few days so the beds were pretty muddy.

The sun was just starting to set as I finished up in the hen house. New bedding meant that the chickens would be warm and dry. I topped up their water and their feed and added an herbal supplement into their feeder. I was just tidying away the containers when I heard tyres on the drive. I peered out of the shed window to see two men, dressed in black getting out of a large black four-wheeler. I could swear that they had guns.

"Al, you check the hut, I'll look in the sheds. We can't leave without that money." I heard one shout to the other. So one was called Al. I wondered what the other one was called. 'The Other One' would have to do for now. They weren't stupid. They knew that the deadline for collecting the money was up. They could also probably guess that, if I had it, I couldn't have banked it. They'd waited until they thought I'd collected it, as that amount of cash would be easier to find than just a code on an SD card.

I ducked down and peered out of the shed window. Al had gone into the cabin and The Other One had started at the greenhouse. If he worked along the garden, he would go to the log store next and then come in here. The door of the hen house faced the cabin. I'd shut the hen house door to keep the draught out as I worked. If I opened it to try to escape, I risked one or both of them seeing me. I heard footsteps outside. The Other One had moved on from the greenhouse. I didn't have long.

I crawled into the space under the chickens. I pushed Philpot's bed and food forward and pulled the boxes in front of me. I just hoped that they wouldn't search behind the boxes. Though I guessed they'd probably search in the boxes for the money. I'd have to stay still and absolutely silent. Just then Philpot came into the shed through the cat flap. He was a bit surprised to see me hunched up where his bed should be so came to investigate. I didn't want him in there. What if they shot him? I tried to push him back out of the cat flap but he made a small meowing protest. That was no good either. I didn't want him making a noise.

I could hear the chickens heading back into their area above me. It was getting dark now, time for them to come home to roost. I hadn't closed the door to the roosting area. One of them was bound to investigate and jump down into the main part of the shed. What if she got hurt too? I just shut my eyes and concentrated on my breathing.

As the two men searched, they kept shouting to each other. There was something oddly familiar about Al's voice but it took me a while to work out where I'd heard it before. At one point, The Other One ribbed him about his choice of footwear and Al replied with a sarcastic

"Well excuse me!" That was the light bulb moment and I realised that he was the person who'd grabbed my elbow in the underpass near the Outlet Village the week before. I suddenly had that cold soup in my stomach moment again. What might have happened if Harry, Sarah, and Tim hadn't turned up when they did? Would I have been kidnapped then? Taken away and beaten until I told them where the money was? Possibly even killed? It occurred to me that Harry, Sarah and Tim had joined an ever-lengthening queue of people claiming to have saved my life.

For some reason, a lot of chicken-keepers give their hens ladies' names such as Henrietta or Philomena. I'd always had hens that had been 'rescued' from intensive egg producing farms. They used to be called battery hens as they were kept in batteries of cages, one in each cage. The system has been outlawed in this country so they are now kept in large sheds or in larger cages with several birds. It's supposed to make them happier and allow them to exhibit normal chicken behaviour. I'm not really sure that I believe that it's any better for them.

The hens tend to look physically similar, sort of orangey brown, a similar colour to a ginger cat, with white speckling on their feathers. When they come out of their confinement they often have very few feathers and are, cruelly, referred to as "oven ready" by the farmers and the rescue team. They peck their feathers out through boredom while they're in the farm sheds. But they soon grow new ones and, within weeks of moving into their new homes, they generally start to behave as chickens should, scratching and pecking and displaying their own little personalities.

I name my chickens after their personalities or their physical characteristics. I'd had this batch for about 18 months now and they'd become Noisy, Jumpy, Runner, Lazy, The Slow One (always last to the treats) and, you'd realise why if you saw her, Big Bird. Big Bird was much bigger than the average hen, sit her beside Philpot and it was difficult to decide who was the larger. She was the top of the pack, bossing the others around, the first to try anything new, letting the others have their turn only after she'd made sure it was up to scratch for them. She reminded me of Gran in a way, always fussing to make sure everything was just so.

What happened next was one of those scenes out of a cartoon, which you see and don't believe would ever happen. A series of coincidences that just doesn't occur in real life. The Other One lifted the latch to the hen house door, which startled Philpot who jumped onto one of the boxes. At the same time, Big Bird realising that the door into their roosting area was open, jumped down onto the box on top of Philpot, who, already tense and frightened, howled loudly and sprung forward just as The Other One walked into the hen house. Big Bird, also startled, also jumped forward, wings flapping and squawking loudly. The Other One was tall, well over six foot, and had to stoop to get in the shed door only to be met, in the half darkness, by an orange ball of screaming fur and feathers. The ball split into two components. Philpot headed straight into The Other One's stomach.

Anyone who's had a cat use their stomach as a springboard will know just how painful it can be and Philpot did just that. With his claws at their fullest extent, he pushed against The Other One's stomach, using it as a surface against which to launch himself off towards his cat flap. Big Bird, who'd tried, but never quite succeeded, at mastering the art of flying, jumped upwards straight into The Other One's face, beak first.

The man, cried out, well more screamed really, and stumbled backwards, his hands over his face. The cat flap rattled furiously making us both jump while Big Bird, who'd landed at his feet, was giving him a good telling off for disturbing her peace. She squawked and pecked angrily at his legs. As he tried to back out of the shed, he fell backwards over the edging of the raised bed into the fresh chicken manure. I could tell from his yelling that his buttocks had found the pink garden claw. The shed door swung shut again.

I literally had to shove my fist into my mouth to keep myself quiet. I'm still not sure whether I would have laughed or screamed. My heart was beating so fast, I was convinced that The Other One would hear it so I shut my eyes and practiced my breathing techniques. I tried not to think of The Other One, annoyed at being attacked by a brace of orange animals, riddling the shed with shot. I wondered where Philpot was but decided that he was probably at the top of a tree halfway to Cirencester by now.

Big Bird, the excitement over, jumped back up to the roosting area and was taking her annoyance out on the feeder. She was pecking at it so loudly, I thought it was the long-anticipated gun shot. I hunched down into my hiding place with my hands over my ears. As if that was going to save me from certain death!

After a few minutes of quiet, I took my hands away from ears and realised that I as still alive. Al must have ascertained that the cabin was empty of both money and me and I heard the two of them talking.

"You go and check that shed if you want to, I'm not going back in there again." That must be The Other One.

"Nah, you're OK. We'll just wait here until the B***** gets back. The Boss wants either the money or the SD card. We just wait for it. We've got all night. You wanted an excuse to get out of going to the in-laws for New Year, now you've got it." Great, now I was trapped in the hen house for eternity. But I did know that they were expecting an SD card, not a piece of paper or any other kind of message.

I sat for a while trying to assess my options but I was well and truly stuck where I was. I risked peeking out of the window. It was nearly dark so I figured they wouldn't be able to see into the shed but I could see them, sat in their car, silhouetted against the streetlights. I couldn't risk opening the shed door, as they'd see it, even in the dark. I live in a densely packed, mostly residential, area so the streetlights stay on all night, unlike some suburbs of Swindon where they're turned off at midnight. As we're also quite high up, we get the glow from the town centre. It's never fully dark here and, even in the dead of night, I can walk up and down my garden without a torch. I frequently go out collecting slugs and snails at night. If I can see slugs without a torch, two men with guns would certainly see me.

I thought about trying to get out of Philpot's cat flap. It was on the side of the shed facing away from the cabin so they might not see me. I discounted that straight away. I might have lost weight since leaving work but I wouldn't even get one leg through that opening, let alone both. I also thought about the pop-hole that the chickens used, that was on the other side of the shed and led out into the run, but it was about the same size as the cat flap. The window was no good, it didn't open so I'd have to break it to get out and they'd hear me.

I continued to sit. My phone was still in the cabin so I couldn't call for help. It had been in my pocket until I made a cup of tea. The cup of tea was still sitting on the shelf above my head. I picked it up and took a sip that I promptly spat out; a mouthful of chicken feathers in cold tea is not an experience I will repeat willingly.

I was beginning to get hungry. All I needed now was for my stomach to rumble just as Al and The Other One walked past. I wondered if there was anything in the shed that I could eat. I had considered storing some produce in there, apples, potatoes, pumpkins, that sort of thing. In the end, I'd put some shelves in the garage instead. To preserve produce for any length of time, you really need to keep it at an even, but cool, temperature. The brick-built garage would give more protection from temperature fluctuations than a wooden shed. All that was in the shed was Philpot's dinner or the chickens' feed. I decided I wasn't hungry after all.

How long had I been in the shed? It was still light when I got trapped so that must have been around 3pm. It was fully dark now and I must have been in here a good couple of hours but my watch said it was only 45 minutes. That couldn't be right, my watch must have stopped? But no, the second hand still swept around and the phosphorus numbers on the dial continued to register the minutes, one at a time. How long would they wait? Would they really stay all night? Would I be trapped here for days? It was already getting cold. Would I get hypothermia? Dying trapped in a hen house wasn't in my life plan. What if I did die? Who would notice? If I didn't turn up to dancing, would anyone there think to come looking for me? I doubted it. It could be days before someone, Rosemary or Alan, concerned that they couldn't reach me on the phone, would come looking. What would they find? Rotting bones, picked clean by very fat chickens?

I thought about climbing into the roosting area with the chickens and cuddling up to them to keep warm. Just at that point, one of the chickens farted very loudly and I heard a large dollop of poop splat down onto the floor of their roosting area above my head. What did I say about being used to the smell? Forget that, I clearly wasn't. Perhaps dying of hypothermia was better than lying in that stench.

Could I send Philpot to alert the neighbours? You heard about dogs fetching help. Could I write a note and attach it to Philpot's collar? Well, that was a non-starter as Philpot didn't wear a collar. Anyway, would Philpot ever forgive me for the trauma he'd experienced when Big Bird landed on him? He didn't seem to be in too much of a hurry to come back to check up on me.

I peered out of the window again but they were still there. I looked at my watch again. Only two minutes had elapsed. This was going to be a long night.

I leant back against a box and it moved slightly. The contents inside shifted and I sat back up. That was the box with the drone in it and I didn't want to break it by leaning on it. But, wait a minute, could I send the drone with a message to one of the neighbours? That was the best idea I'd had so far. I could probably, just about, get the drone out of the cat flap if I angled it correctly. Would there be enough light for me to see where it was going?

Probably not but did that matter? I just needed to get a piece of paper with a message to someone, anyone. Did I have any paper? No, but I had some seed marker labels in a pot on the shelf, and a pencil to write on the labels. There was some string as well. I could tie labels onto the drone's feet, put it outside the cat flap and send it towards Gloucester Road. Someone was bound to find it. Maybe I could use the camera on the drone to communicate with that person using some form of Morse Code? If only I'd learned Morse Code.

I started to unpack the box when a thought struck me. Had I recharged its batteries since I last used it? No, they were completely flat. I was just about to despair when something else caught my eye; the netbook was in the same box. Slowly I picked it up. Please let its batteries have some charge. I opened it up and switched it on, praying that it was on mute and wouldn't play that irritating Windows tune as it warmed up. It took forever for the screen to come on. I angled it away from the window. I didn't want Al and The Other One to see the glow.

While it warmed up, I tried to think through what I should do. The netbook was too slow for Skype or Facetime. I wasn't sure if I'd set up Facebook on it. If I hadn't then I doubted I could remember the password. I'd been using it for e-mail so I knew that would work. I'd try e-mailing someone first, and then try logging in to Facebook. But who to contact? Alan was a bit of a technophobe, only checking his e-mails once a day. Besides he'd probably go all Bruce Willis and charge over here to take on the gunmen himself getting shot in the process. My neighbours were all elderly and I didn't relish the thought of giving any of them a heart attack. I didn't want to upset Alison, and Rosemary was at her in-laws. I started to think about other friends, but discounted each one in turn for different reasons. Eddie was a possibility as she wouldn't panic, but she'd probably think it was a wind-up. We'd played too many practical jokes on each other in the past.

For once (or should I say yet again) I was lucky. The netbook was both on mute and had a little bit of charge but I didn't have my phone to tether it to. Could I pick up someone's unlocked Wifi? I searched for an open Wifi and found one called Home Street Academy. It was locked so I counted on them changing the password at the start of the new term, not the end of the old. I typed 'Examtime' into the box and waited. It worked, the netbook screen opened to the school's homepage.

I logged in to my e-mails and watched the new ones roll into my inbox. The last one came from Katherine the Surveyor. She'd promised to send me a list of approved builders in my area and she'd done just that. The e-mail had only been sent a couple of seconds ago. She was online and I knew she wouldn't be flustered.

Changing the message header to 'Help call the police – this is not a joke' I replied:

'Please help, I repeat, this is not a joke and my account has not been hacked. Two men with guns have come to the cabin looking for me. I am hiding in the hen house. Please call Detective Keith Washington or PC William Barrett at Gable Cross police station. The gunmen are connected to the lowlife we saw scavenging my house when we first met – Sam'. I hoped the last sentence would convince her that it was really me and that I genuinely was in danger.

When I say that the netbook had a little bit of charge, it was only a very little bit. As I pressed send the screen died. I could only hope that it had managed to send the message before it switched off.

I imagined Katherine Longthorn receiving the message. She would raise her eyebrows and then, without a moment's hesitation, pick up her phone. She probably already had Detective Keith's number on speed dial, so she would call him immediately and relay my message in a very matter of fact way. I checked my watch. It was only 20 past four. It felt like I'd been trapped for weeks but I'd only been in here for a little over an hour. I took comfort from the fact that I'd been to the loo when I stopped for a cuppa – that tingling in my bladder must just be my brain playing tricks on me.

My brain carried on playing tricks. When the police didn't turn up straight away I imagined Katherine sending her e-mail to me. Then closing her laptop, getting up from her desk and heading home. She would put her phone in her handbag and ignore it until she got back to work on the 2nd. Then it would be too late. I'd either be dead or, well, dead.

I thought of another plan. The SD card was still in the netbook. I looked at it. Perhaps I should just surrender? What would happen if I gave the card to the gunmen? Obviously, they were going to thank me nicely take it, go away and never bother me again. Obviously, they weren't. They'd make me fire up a device to view the SD card. As soon as they saw it was blank, they'd know that I'd taken the money. They'd force me to hand over the details of the money's location at gunpoint and then they'd shoot me. They might spin it out until they'd collected the money. I suspected that Sainsbury's in

Stroud closed early on New Year's Eve so they'd probably keep me trapped, tied up somewhere like Jimmy's brother, until one of them could collect the money. As soon as they had it, they'd shoot me.

I leant back against the wall of the hen house. Whichever way things went. I was doomed.

I checked my watch again. All of that worrying had occupied my mind for a little over two minutes.

I tried to get my brain back to imagining Katherine calling Detective Keith. I played out step-by-step what would happen; trying to work out, in real time, how long each step would take. Perhaps she didn't have his number? Perhaps she had to look up the number for Gable Cross police station? Perhaps the station only had a skeleton staff on and it took them a while to answer? Perhaps they didn't believe her and it took a while for her to persuade them? This is Swindon after all. Things like that just don't happen here. Perhaps they wouldn't tie me too tightly and I'd be able to escape during the night? Perhaps they'd kill me straight away? Perhaps…

Perhaps those are blue flashing lights I can see through the shed window? Perhaps those are sirens I can hear? Perhaps those screeching tyres are police cars pulling up the drive? Perhaps those shouts are Al and The Other One, trying to escape?

I waited. I didn't dare look out of the window, in case I was imagining it all. After an age, the shed door opened. The chickens had all settled down for the night so there were no more flying Big Birds. Just as well. I wouldn't have been in PC William's good books if he'd been attacked by one of my chickens. He called to me "Sam, are you there? It's PC William Barrett."

I slowly crawled out of my hiding space. I'd been sitting still for so long my back had seized up so I ended up tumbling out of the cramped space. PC William caught me and we ended up in a funny sort of awkward embrace. He stood me upright and shone a light in my face.

"You hurt?"

"No – apart from a stiff back and a desperate need for the loo."

"It's safe, on you go."

I dashed back to the cabin, past a couple of uniformed police who stood back when PC William shouted to them to let me pass. I'd never been so relieved to be relieved.

Aftermath

Al and The Other One were led away in handcuffs. Police boots trampled on my parsnips, and they left the greenhouse door open, despite it already being below freezing. Eventually, the uniformed police, happy that there weren't any more armed intruders lurking in the brassicas, left. It was just Detective Keith and myself. He was making notes.

"Have you released Wendy's father yet?" I asked.

"Not yet. We've got permission to hold him for another 48 hours while we follow up on information that he's given us."

"What about the cousin, have you arrested him yet for leaking details about the evidence?"

Detective Keith sat up and looked at me out of the corner of his eye, as if he was assessing how much he could trust me.

"No. We're waiting. We think he might be leaking information on another case as well. We're going to try to trap him when he gets back to work in the New Year. But that's not to go any further."

"Understood." I nodded.

I changed the subject. "I bet this has mucked up your plans for New Year? Do you have to write this up tonight?"

"No worries, police don't get New Year's Eve off. Even detectives."

He paused and looked back over his notes. 'They definitely said an SD card?" He asked for about the fifth time.

"Yes."

"And they definitely didn't say what they were expecting to find on the SD card?"

"No, I mean yes, the definitely didn't say."

"And you definitely don't know anything about this SD card?"

I had tried every trick in the book not to look him in the eye but this was the fifth time he'd asked me about the SD card so I fronted it out. I looked him straight in the eye, raised my eyebrows, breathed out through my nose, shook my head and said "No – the only SD card I have is the one in the camera that I showed you just now." It turned out that the card with the risqué photographs that I was thinking of must have ended up in E.J.'s camera. Mine just had innocent holiday shots and a few photos of Philpot as a kitten.

He looked at me, almost apologetic but somehow not quite apologetic enough. "I'm sorry, Sam, but we are going to have to search the house ruins again but we're also going to have to search here and the garden, just in case."

I sagged back into my chair. "Tonight?"

Detective Keith snorted: "On New Year's Eve, for a case that isn't even a murder case, in a house of a witness, not a suspect? Ha, no. I'd never square that one. Unlikely to be tomorrow either, given it's a bank holiday. It'll probably be next week before we can get a team out here. Don't worry, I'll call before we come out. If you do find anything, I'm sure I can trust you to hand it in – can't I?"

"Of course," I beamed.

"Have you got somewhere to stay? You shouldn't be on your own tonight." That seemed to have become the chorus of the theme tune to the pantomime that was my life nowadays.

I assured him I wouldn't be on my own but I waited a full five minutes after he'd gone before I stood on the doorstep and whistled.

Hiding the evidence

Alan and Rhona thought it was hilarious that I could call Philpot like a dog. I just whistled and he came. It's not true that you can't train cats. You just have to convince them that there's something in it for them. I'd trained him right from a kitten that if he responded to a whistle he would get a treat. This time was no exception. It took a few minutes for him to trust me enough to return for his chicken flavoured Munchie-Chewie. At first I wondered if he would think that anything chicken-flavoured would be a treat after his run in with Big Bird, but he attacked it with venom. I'd better make sure that the door to the chickens' apartment in the shed was firmly shut in future.

He obviously hadn't been up a tree. Once again he was covered in cobwebs, which made me think that he'd probably been hiding indoors somewhere, possibly next-door's log store. A germ of an idea started to sprout in my mind. I laid back on the futon and thought back to that first morning in the cabin.

Philpot jumped up beside me and started to wash off the cobwebs. It had been the thought of arachnid induced, feline vomit that had got me up off the futon that time and it was the thought of vomit that got me up off the futon again this time.

I needed to ensure that the drug dealers knew I didn't have the SD card. The easiest way to do that was to make sure that they knew the police had it. How could I get it to the police without anyone being suspicious that I'd had it all along?

I'd already decided that I wasn't going to the dance tonight. I should have gone, of course. It would have taken my mind off everything that had happened and I wouldn't have been alone, but I knew that I wouldn't be able to concentrate. I knew that I would be Lindihopping when I should be Cerocing, that my Rock and Roll would morph into a Cha Cha Cha and that I would end up in a Salsa hold instead of a Ballroom hold. Besides, I wasn't sure that the minion fancy dress costume I'd made from the Liverpool fan's blue bed linen, really fitted me all that well.

All I really wanted to do tonight was eat the lamb casserole, which was gradually congealing in the slow cooker, and wallow in the horror of what had happened. For that I needed alcohol.

Putting on my coat and gloves, I accompanied Philpot to the cabin door. But I didn't head straight to the shops, instead I went first to the hen house. Swapping my knitted, weather-proof gloves for a pair of cheap latex ones, the sort that you get free from any petrol station, I extracted the SD card from the netbook.

First I wiped it with acetone to remove any of my fingerprints. Then I washed it in the water butt outside the shed to remove any traces of the acetone and replace them with rainwater. After that, I put it down on the concrete path and smashed the sharp end of a spade into it. I'd hoped to break it in two but I just succeeded in cracking it. I'd have to sharpen the spade before I could use it again but I figured that would be worth the effort.

After all this, I hoped that the SD card would be sufficiently damaged that the forensics experts wouldn't bother trying to recover any files from it. That way they wouldn't realise it had already been wiped. It would ruin my plans if they realised that someone had tampered with it.

Changing back into my cold weather gloves, I headed off through the garden, past my ruined house, towards Gloucester Road. As I got to the end of my drive I bent down to do up my shoelace. Under the cover of darkness, I dug the card into the mud at the bottom of Jack and Linda's drive and pulled it back out again. I wanted to cover it in the sort of muck that you get on a busy road: mud, tyre rubber, diesel fumes, that sort of thing. I walked a few steps down the road to the crossing. I could have gone to Farmer's Fayre but that was on my side of the road. I needed an excuse to cross at the crossing so Pedro's Off License was my destination. I stopped and waited for the traffic. The road was getting busy with people off to their New Year's parties. That suited me just fine. I crossed to the central refuge and waited again as cars went past. There was a short gap in the traffic so I sprinted to the other side, dropping the card as I did so. I turned as I reached the pavement, just in time to see a car wheel drive over the card and flip it to the side of the road. Perfect.

I nodded to Pedro as I entered his store. He always stayed open on New Year's Eve to take advantage of the last minute trade in party essentials. We chatted for a while as I paid for a couple of bottles of Old Speckled Hen, after the run in with Big Bird, I thought it an appropriate choice of beer, a bottle of cheap prosecco to see in the New Year, a big bag of Doritos, and the largest bar of chocolate Pedro had. It was comfort food that I needed.

I walked slowly back to the cabin. At the crossing, I noticed that the SD card was still sitting at the edge of the road. There was a crack between the surface of the road and the kerbstone of the central refuge. As I crossed, I kicked the card into that crack so that it was only just visible. I knew all those practice sessions at football would come in useful one day. Back at the cabin, I drank half a bottle of Old Speckled Hen and started on the lamb while I summoned up the courage to pick up the phone.

"Hello Sam, what can I do for you?" Detective Keith asked.

"Hi. Can I check something? When the forensic team were here did they look at the crossing where Markus Stallbrigg threw up?"

Detective Keith considered for a moment and then said: "No. There was vomit on the side of the lorry. At that point we just wanted to test it for evidence of narcotics. Why?"

"I was following him as he came round the corner. He leant pretty far out of the cab when he threw up. It was what caused the lorry to start swerving and the crash to happen. What if he dropped the SD card then?" I hadn't really needed to say that last sentence; I could hear Detective Keith jumping to his feet before I got that far.

"I'll meet you at the crossing in twenty minutes." Came the response.

To make myself late for the meeting, I finished my lamb, and the beer, and started on the chocolate. I needed it for courage. Chocolate works far better in that respect than alcohol in my opinion. All of the high but you get to keep your wits about you.

Detective Keith was already at the crossing with a couple of other police officers when I got there. They'd coned off the eastbound side of the road and an officer in uniform was directing traffic around the other side of the central refuge. The other officer, wearing white, paper overalls, was down on his hands and knees with a light strapped to his head, searching.

"Sorry I'm late." I breathed over Detective Keith, hoping he'd smell the beer and think that I was drunker than I really was. It would give me an excuse to have lost track of time and be late. That way he would see that I hadn't just dropped the card (which of course I actually had).

"Have you found anything?"

He was holding a white plastic box and showed me the contents. Two neatly labelled plastic bags. One contained a ring pull from a can, the other one an unidentifiable mass of what looked like mud and leaves.

"Not much so far."

We watched in silence as the officer in the white overalls carried on searching. Detective Keith obviously felt himself to be above crawling around on a muddy road looking for evidence.

Cold and bored, I started to walk towards the junction with Chene Street. Detective Keith followed me.

"Talk me through what happened," he suggested as we walked down Chene Street a few yards.

"This was about where I caught up with him. He'd been speeding from the Home Street roundabout but slowed down when he got here. Not much, not enough to make the turn."

I pointed to the bin on the corner that he'd swiped. We both walked across and peered in as if, miraculously, the SD card would be there a month later. I looked up at him and raised my eyebrows: "It's not going to be in there is it?"

We slowly walked back around the corner towards the crossing as I talked through step-by-step or, should I say, wheel revolution by wheel revolution, what had happened. "This was where he mounted the pavement. That was where he leant out of the cab."

Just as we approached the crossing, White Overalls shot his hand up. "Over here!"

Detective Keith ran over. The other police officer glanced round but was trying to sort out traffic heading at him from both directions so turned back to what he was doing.

Detective Keith looked at where White Overalls was pointing. In a small gap between the surface of the road and the kerbstone of the central refuge something black could just about be seen in the beam of the torch on his forehead. Detective Keith took several photographs and then nodded to White Overalls who took a pair of tweezers and extracted the SD card. He stood up and inspected it. It was almost in two parts now. If you shook it, the two halves would fall apart. He carefully placed it in its own plastic bag in the box.

The two policemen looked at each other and then White Overalls uttered the words that I'd hoped beyond hope that I would hear: "It looks pretty beaten up. We won't be able to get anything off that one."

One year on

30th November, one year after the crash. I'm still living in the cabin and facing another winter here but that's actually rather OK. It's a great little home and I've kitted it out to a standard worthy of posting it on Pinterest; one of those "Swindon resident turns tiny shed into cosy home" sorts of posts.

Life has taken quite an unexpected turn. I went back to the school for the launch of their campaign "Don't be an ass, don't be a mule." It really was quite good, so good in fact, that other schools have copied the idea. I now work, on a voluntary basis, with about a dozen schools helping them to develop and run social media campaigns. At first it was just about drugs but they've broadened the themes out now. I'm currently working with a school in Weston-Super-Mare on a campaign about reducing the amount of plastic in the sea.

Although I don't get paid for it, the satisfaction of helping the youngsters is enormous. I contacted Stan and Lydia in Bristol and explained to them that I wanted to do this and they said it was a great idea. I should use the money in the Just Giving account for the travel expenses. It takes up a about two days a month and the great thing about working with schools is that each year there is a fresh new market to tap into. I'm going back to the Home Street Academy next week to meet the new group of 16- and 17-year-olds to talk about their campaign ideas. In return, they keep me up to date with the latest technologies and developments in social media.

Through the drugs campaign, I was introduced to a local charity that helps recovering drug addicts by giving them training in life skills. Twice a week, I go along to their centre to give talks and demonstrations on gardening. There is a small courtyard at the back so, together, we plant and grow flowers and herbs in pots. It seems to work and the charity has a very good success rate at helping addicts stay away from their drug of choice.

The insurance money came through in full in late January and the mortgage used to fund the flats was paid off. I had just enough insurance money left to pay for a timber-frame house kit from one of the suppliers recommended by Katherine the Surveyor. But the kit is only a small part of the rebuild cost so I'm doing as much of the rest as I can myself. Alan helps, of course, when he's not working, but he's going to have a lot less time soon. He and Rhona got back together at New Year and they're expecting a little girl next summer. Maybe I'll be a godparent? It'll be nice to have an excuse to buy pretty, feminine things. All of the other children around me are boys so I don't get a chance. I just hope that she isn't like most of the rest of the girls in my family, tomboys who are in to practical rather than pretty.

Alison's in remission now and she and Barry celebrated with a cruise around the Norwegian Fjords. Barry's obviously not lost his love of travelling but now he takes his wife with him. They're off to Australia for a month after Christmas.

I gave evidence at the inquests into the deaths of Markus Stalbrigg and Wendy Watson. The first was ruled as death by misadventure and the second accidental. Neither went into the details of the drugs connection.

The kidnapping wasn't even mentioned during Wendy's inquest.

Niall and Jimmy were cautioned and released. They were reprimanded by their employer but kept their jobs in the under-staffed NHS.

Al and The Other One admitted to charges of brandishing a dangerous weapon and breaking and entering. As they'd pleaded guilty, there wasn't a full trial, just a sentencing, so I didn't need to appear to give evidence.

Josh Watson is currently awaiting trial in Bristol on several drugs charges and his cousin is serving a year for perverting the course of justice. It's been a busy old year in the courts of the South West.

The income I get from the flats, now free of mortgage repayment, is just enough to pay for the materials and labour I need to help get the house done. It's a slow process but I'm enjoying it. Kevin McCloud wouldn't be impressed, it's just a standard kit house, but it's my standard kit house and I'm proud of it. I'm hoping to be in for next Christmas but don't they all say that?

I live a very frugal, eco-friendly life now. Something I wouldn't have the time to do if I was working. I grow all my own fruit and vegetables, organically, and I still get a good supply of eggs. I swapped my apples for cider again and had a go at making my own wine. I joined the crew at dancing which means that, in exchange for sitting at the desk and taking the subscriptions, I get to go to all the classes and dances for free. I became treasurer of the Chene Street amateur football club, which allows me to go to practice for free. I doubt I'll ever make the team but it's great exercise and keeps me in touch with my mates.

I did start doing up old furniture and bric-a-brac and selling it at vintage fairs. I'll never become rich doing it but I do get to add a bit to the bank account once a month or so. It's just enough to convince anyone who's looking into my finances too deeply that I have enough income to live on. I sold the salvageable roof tiles to a guy in the next street that was building an extension and wanted tiles to match the existing ones. I chopped up the floorboards, staircase and doorframes for firewood. I rescued the doors to re-use in the new house and recycled some of the windows to build another greenhouse. The good bricks were used to edge more vegetable beds in the kitchen garden and the radiators and copper pipes were sold for scrap. As I said before, nothing much gets wasted around here.

Each month I allow myself to withdraw £500 from the Bank of Cat and Chickens. I picked up the money from Sainsbury's in Stroud. I couldn't think of a way of getting it into the banking system without drawing attention to it, so I had to find somewhere to hide it. Al and The Other One may be in prison but the cabin isn't secure enough to hold that much money.

If you happen to look inside a fictional hen house on a patch of land that doesn't exist, off a street that was never built, you'll see an old kitchen cabinet in the space under the chickens' apartment, next to Philpot's bed. If, like me, you're a fan of life hack posts on the web, you'll probably have seen pictures of drawers hidden behind the plinth under such cabinets. Pull the drawer out and you'll find it full of old black sacks, and empty feed and compost bags. You never know when they might come in useful.

But pull that drawer right out and you'll find another, narrower, drawer behind. Glance in there and you'll find some mouldy newspaper and a large population of spiders. Summon up the courage to lift the newspaper and the spiders and there are some rusty biscuit tins, the sort that were being sold off cheaply in the Swindon Outlet Village in the New Year sales. Inside those tins, in plastic sandwich bags, each containing £500, is the balance of the cash, mostly in £20 notes.

If I'm careful that should last me as spending money for long enough to get the house finished and a good few years afterwards. It's only fair, really, that the drugs dealers should pay for wrecking my home, kidnapping me, and keeping me prisoner in a shed, not to mention the amount of time I spent giving evidence and sorting out the mess they created. Besides, I couldn't do my voluntary work with the schools or the drugs charity if I had to go back to paid employment.

There is just one fly that landed in the ointment as I was watching the breakfast news this morning. I was drinking my coffee and eating my home-grown scrambled eggs when Naga Munchetty looked straight at me and introduced the next article: "Now we are going live to the Treasury where Steph is going to show us the new £20 note that is being introduced next year. The old ones will cease to be legal tender in six months' time. Over to you Steph."

The End

Reading Group Questions

1. Is Sam short for Samantha or Samuel? What is it about the story that influenced your decision?

2. Would it have mattered if you had known from the start that Sam was the opposite gender from what you think? Would you have enjoyed the book as much?

3. Do you think Sam is a good person?

4. Was Sam right to keep the money?